He kissed her again, long and deep and achingly gentle.

"This is it, Joanna," he warned as he drew away again to watch her lashes flutter upward to reveal eyes dazed by a hopeless passion. "So keep looking at me," he urged. "For this is what I am now. Not the guy who crept stealthily around your problems the way I did the last time we were together—but this man. The one who means to invade your defensive space at every opportunity. And do you know why? Because each time I do it, you quiver with pleasure more."

"I can never be a proper wife to you."

"You think so?" Sandro pondered. "Well, we shall see...."

MICHELLE REID

The Marriage Surrender

Passion™

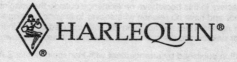

HARLEQUIN®

TORONTO • NEW YORK • LONDON
AMSTERDAM • PARIS • SYDNEY • HAMBURG
STOCKHOLM • ATHENS • TOKYO • MILAN • MADRID
PRAGUE • WARSAW • BUDAPEST • AUCKLAND

ISBN 0-373-12014-1

THE MARRIAGE SURRENDER

First North American Publication 1999.

Copyright © 1998 by Michelle Reid.

Printed in U.S.A.

CHAPTER ONE

'COULD I s-speak to Alessandro Bonetti, please?'

The public call box smelled of stale cigarettes. Pale-faced, the full length of her slender body muscle-locked by the mettle she needed to make this telephone call, Joanna barely noticed the smell or the unsavoury mess littering the floor beneath her black-booted feet as she stood there clutching the telephone receiver to her ear.

'Who is calling, please?' a coolly concise female voice enquired.

'I'm...' she began—then stopped, white teeth pressing into her full bottom lip as the answer to that question stuck firmly in her throat.

She couldn't say it. She just could not bring herself to reveal her true identity to anyone but Alessandro himself when there was a very good chance that he might refuse to speak to her, and in the present state that she was in, she didn't need some cold-voiced telephonist listening to that little humiliation.

She had been there before...

'It—it's a personal call,' she temporised, closing her eyes on a faint prayer that the reply was enough to get her access to the great man himself.

It wasn't. 'I'm afraid I will have to have your name,' the voice insisted, 'before I can enquire if Mr Bonetti is available to speak to you.'

Well, at least that stone-walling response placed Sandro in the country. Joanna made a grim note. She had half expected him to have gone back to live and work in Rome by now.

'Then put me through to his secretary,' she demanded, 'and I'll discuss this further with her.'

There was a pause, one of those taut ones, packed with silent pique at Joanna's rigidly determined tone. Then, 'Please hold,' the voice clipped at her, and the line went quiet.

The seconds began to tick slowly by, taking with them the desperation that had managed to bring her this far. A desperation that had kept her awake last night, trying to come up with some other way to get herself out of this mess without having to involve Sandro. But every which way she'd tried to look at it, it had always come down to two straight choices.

Arthur Bates or Sandro.

A shudder ripped through her, the mere thought of Arthur Bates' name enough to keep her hanging onto that telephone line, when every self-preserving instinct she possessed was telling her to cut loose and make a bolt into hiding somewhere rather than resort to this.

But she was tired of hiding. Tired of—being this person who stood on her own, isolated by her own inability to reach out to another human being and simply ask for help.

So, here she was, she reminded herself bracingly, ready to ask for that help. Ready to reach out to the only human being she felt she could reach out to. If Sandro said No, get lost, then she would. But she had to give him one last chance—give *herself* this chance to put her life back together again.

After all, she consoled herself, against the fretful doubts rattling around inside her head, she wasn't intending dumping permanently on him, was she? She was simply going to put a proposition to him, get his answer, then get the hell out of his life again.

For good. That would be part of her proposition. Help me this one time and I promise never to bother you again.

Easy. Nothing to it. Sandro wasn't a monster. He was, in actual fact, quite a decent human being. He couldn't still be feeling bitter towards her, surely? Not after all this time.

Then the telephone suddenly began demanding more money and her self-consolation died a death as a much more familiar panic soared abruptly into life, gushing through her system like a raging flood.

What am I doing? she asked herself frantically. *Why* am I doing this?

You're doing this because you've got no damned choice! her mind snapped back, so angrily that it jerked her into urgent movement. Her trembling fingers reached out towards the small stack of coins she had piled up in front of her ready to feed into the pay box. She made a grab for the top coin in the stack—and stupidly sent the rest of them scattering so they fell in a chinking shower to the ground.

'Oh, damn it,' she muttered, starting to bend to pick up the scattered coins as a voice suddenly sounded down the earpiece.

'Good morning, Mr Bonetti's secretary speaking,' it announced. 'How may I help you?'

The voice made her shoot upright again. 'Just a minute,' she muttered, struggling to feed the only coin she had stopped from falling into the required slot with fingers that decidedly shook. The line cleared and Joanna took another few moments to pull her ragged nerves together. 'I w-would like to speak to Mr—to Alessandro, please.' She quickly changed tack, hoping the personal touch might get her past this next obstruction.

It didn't. 'I'm afraid I must insist on your name,' Sandro's secretary maintained.

Her name. Her teeth gritted together, eyes closing on a fresh bout of indecision. Now what did she do? she asked herself pensively. Tell the truth? Let this woman bear witness to the full depth of Sandro's refusal, instead of the other cool voice she had spoken to before?

'This is—M-Mrs Bonetti,' she heard herself mumble, the name sounding as strange leaving her own lips as it must have sounded to the woman on the other end of the telephone line.

There was a short sharp pause. Then, '*Mrs* Bonetti?' the voice repeated. 'Mrs *Alessandro* Bonetti?'

'Yes,' Joanna confirmed, not blaming the woman for sounding so astonished. Joanna herself had never managed to come to terms with being that particular person. 'Will you ask Alessandro if he has a few minutes he could spare for me, please?'

'Of course,' his secretary instantly agreed.

The line went quiet again. Joanna breathed an unsteady sigh into the mouthpiece, wondering how many cats she was setting loose amongst Sandro's little pigeons by daring to make an announcement like that.

Again she waited, so tense now she could barely unclench her jaw-bone, the thrumming silence setting her foot tapping on the debris-littered concrete base of the call box, fingernails doing the same against the metal casing of the telephone. And there was a man standing just outside the kiosk, obviously waiting to use the telephone after her. He kept on sending her impatient glances and her palms felt sweaty; she tried running them one at a time down her denim-clad thighs but it didn't make any difference, they still felt sweaty.

'Mrs Bonetti?'

'Yes?' The single word shot like a bullet from her tension-locked throat.

'Mr Bonetti is in conference at the moment.' The voice sounded incredibly guarded all of a sudden. 'But he said for you to leave your number and he will call you back as soon as he is free.'

'I can't do that,' Joanna said, feeling a dragging sense

of relief and a contrary wave of despair go sweeping through her. 'I mean—I'm in a public call box and...'

Shaky fingers came up to push agitatedly through the long silken fall of her red-gold hair while she tried to think quickly with a brain that didn't want to think at all. Sandro couldn't speak to her and she didn't think she could accumulate enough courage to do this again.

'I'll h-have to call him back,' she stammered out finally, grasping at straws that really weren't straws at all, but simply excuses to stop this before it soared out of all control. 'Tell him I'll call him back s-some time w-when I—' Her excuses dried up. 'Goodbye,' she abruptly concluded, and went to replace the telephone.

But, 'No! Mrs Bonetti!' The secretary's voice whipped down the line at her. 'Please wait!' she said urgently. 'Mr Bonetti wants to know your reply before you... Just hold the line a moment longer—please...'

It was a plea—an anxious plea, which was the only thing that stopped Joanna from slamming down the receiver and getting out of there.

That and the fact that she had just had a revolting vision of Arthur Bates smiling at her like a very fat cat who was about to taste the cream. She shuddered again, feeling sick, feeling dizzy, feeling so uptight and confused now that she really didn't know what she wanted to do.

Oh God. She closed her eyes, tried to get a hold on her swiftly decaying reason. Sandro or Arthur Bates? her mind kept on prodding at her. Arthur Bates or Sandro? The choice that was no choice.

Sandro...

Sandro, the man she had not allowed herself to make any contact with for two long wretched years.

Except when she'd told him about Molly, she then remembered, feeling what was left of the colour drain from her cheeks as poor Molly's face swam painfully into her mind. She had tried to contact Sandro once—about Molly.

He had ignored her call for help then, she grimly reminded herself. So there was every chance that he was going to do the same now.

And why not? she derided. There was nothing left between them any more, hadn't been for a long, long—

The phone began demanding more money again. She jumped like a startled deer, eyes flicking open to search a little wildly for another coin. It was only then that she remembered that she had knocked them all flying to the ground a few minutes earlier, and she bent down, functioning on pure instinct now because intelligence seemed to have completely deserted her.

But then, it always did when it came to Sandro, she acknowledged ruefully as her fingers scrambled amongst the dirt, cigarette ends and God alone knew what else that was littering the call box floor.

'Mrs Bonetti?'

'Yes,' she gasped.

'I'm putting you through to Mr Bonetti now...'

There was a crackling sound in her ear that made her wince. Her scrambling fingers discovered one of her missing coins. Grabbing at it, she straightened, face flushed now, breathing gone haywire, fingers fumbling as she attempted to push home the coin, the stupid panic turning her into a quivering, useless mess because she was about to hear Sandro's dark velvet voice again and she didn't know if she could bear it!

The man outside the call box got fed up with waiting and banged angrily on the glass. Joanna turned on him like a mad woman, her blue eyes flashing him a blinding glare of protest.

'Joanna?'

And that was all it took for everything to come crashing down around her—the agitation, the panic—all crowding in and congealing into one seething ball of chest-tightening anguish.

He sounded gruff, he sounded terse, but oh, so familiar that her own voice locked itself into her throat. The man outside banged again; she closed her eyes and set her teeth and felt Sandro's tension sizzle down the telephone line towards her, felt his impatience, his reluctance to accept this call.

'Joanna?' he repeated tersely. Then, 'Damn it!' she heard him curse. 'Are you still there?'

'Yes,' she answered breathlessly, and knew she had just taken one of the biggest, bravest steps of her life with that one tiny word of confirmation. 'S-sorry.' She apologised for the tense delay in taking it, and tried to relax her jaw in an effort to find some semblance of calm. 'I dropped my m-money on the call box f-floor and couldn't find it,' she explained. 'And there's a m-man standing outside w-waiting to use the telephone. He keeps banging on the glass and I—'

The rest was cut off—by herself, because she realised on a wave of despair that she was babbling like an idiot.

Sandro must have been thinking the exact same thing because his tone was tight when he muttered, 'What the hell are you talking about?'

'Sorry,' she whispered again, which seemed to infuriate him.

'I am in the middle of an important meeting here,' he snapped. 'So do you think you could get to the point of this—unexpected—honour?'

Sarcasm, hard and tight. Her eyes closed again, her chest so cramped she could barely drag air into her lungs as each angry word hit her exactly where it was aimed to hit.

'I n-need...'

What did she need? she then stopped to wonder. She had become so addled by now that her reason for calling him at all had suddenly got lost in the ferment of her panic.

'I n-need...' Moistening her dry lips, she tried again. 'Your—advice about something,' she hedged, knowing she couldn't just tell him outright that the only reason she was phoning him after all this time was to ask for money! 'Do you think you could possibly m-meet me somewhere, s-so we can talk?'

No reply. Her nerve-ends reached snapping point. A tight, prickling feeling began to scramble its way up from her tingling toes to her hairline. She couldn't breathe, she couldn't swallow, and, worse than all of that, she felt like weeping.

And if Sandro knew that he would fall off his chair in shock, she mocked herself.

'I am flying to Rome this evening,' he informed her brusquely. 'And my day is fully taken up with meetings until I leave for the airport. It will have to wait until I get back next week.'

'No!' That wouldn't do! 'I can't wait that long. I...' Her voice trailed away, her mind flying off in another direction as she bit into her bottom lip on a fresh wave of desperation. Then, defeatedly, she whispered, 'It doesn't m-matter. I'm s-sorry to have—'

'Don't you damn well dare put that phone down on me!' Sandro warned on an angry growl that told her that, even after all this time, he could still read her intentions like an open book.

And she could hear him muttering something to himself—cursing most likely—in Italian, because Sandro always did revert to his native tongue when he was really angry. She could even see him in full detail while he did it. Tall and lean, an unbearably handsome Latin dark figure, with brown velvet eyes that turned black when angry and a beautifully shaped intensely sensual mouth that could kiss like no mouth she had ever experienced, but could also spit all sorts at her without her knowing what the words were—but, hell, did she get their drift!

Then, emerging from the middle of all that Latin temperament, came a warning beep that the phone needed feeding yet again.

'I haven't any more money!' she gasped into the mouthpiece while her eyes flickered anxiously across the dirty floor at her feet. 'I'll have to—'

'Give me your number!' Sandro snapped.

'But there's a man waiting to use the telephone. I have to—'

'*Maledizione!*' he cursed. 'The number, Joanna!'

She gave it. Her time ran out and the line went dead. She dropped the receiver back onto its rest, then just stood there staring at it, unsure if Sandro had managed to get down every digit before they were cut off, scared that he had done, and terrified that he had not!

Almost faint with stress and wretched confusion, she bent again to search the grubby ground for her other lost coins, found them, then stepped out of the call box to let the man waiting outside take his turn on the telephone.

He sidled past her as though she was some kind of freak. She didn't blame him; if he had been watching her enact her nervous breakdown inside that telephone box, then she knew she must have *looked* like a freak!

Sandro's fault; it was always Sandro's fault when she went to pieces like this. No one else could make her lose all her usually ice-cold self-possession as completely he could. And he had been doing it since the first time she ever set eyes on him. A few short minutes of his undivided company, and he had always been able to turn her into a shivering, quivering wreck of a useless creature.

Sex.

That single telling word hit her with a hard, cruel honesty. The difference between Sandro and every other man she had ever met was the fact that he was the only one who could stir her up sexually.

And that was why she was standing here, a shivering, quivering wreck. Because in stirring her up sexually he also stirred up all the phobias that sent her into this kind of panic.

Fear was the main thing: a stark, staring fear that if she ever gave in to the sex then her life would be over.

Because he would know then, wouldn't he? Know what she was and despise her for it.

The man came out of the phone box. He hadn't been much more than a couple of minutes, which made her feel even guiltier for keeping him waiting as long as she had.

'I'm so sorry I was so long,' she felt compelled to say. 'Only I had difficulty—'

The phone inside the kiosk began to ring and she made a sudden desperate lurch for it, forgetting about the man, forgetting everything as she snatched the receiver to her ear again.

'What the hell happened?' Sandro's voice shot down the line at her. 'I have been trying that number for the last five minutes and kept getting an engaged signal! Were you stupid enough to hold onto the receiver instead of hanging up and waiting for me to call you back?'

Well, Joanna thought ruefully, that just about said it. Stupid. He thought her *that* stupid, and Sandro suffered fools as most people suffered raging toothache.

'I let the man I told you was waiting use the phone,' she explained.

Another of those Italian curses hit her burning eardrums, then she heard him take in a deep breath of air and his voice, when it came again, was more as it should be, grim but controlled.

'What is it you want from me, Joanna,' he demanded. 'Since when have you *ever* wanted anything from me?'

Which only showed that even when he was under control he still couldn't resist another dig at her.

'It isn't something I can discuss over the telephone,' she told him. Then as her own temper suddenly flared, 'And if this is a taste of how your attitude is going to be, then it probably isn't worth me taking it any further!'

'OK—OK,' he conceded on a heavy sigh. 'So I am reacting badly. But I am up to my neck in work at the moment, and the last thing I expected, on top of it all, was for my long-lost *wife* to give me a call!'

'Try for sarcasm,' she snapped. 'Pleasantries just don't become you somehow.'

Their simultaneous sighs were acknowledgements that they both recognised they were reacting to each other now as they had always used to do: biting and scratching.

'How can I help you?' he asked, with more heaviness than hostility.

And Joanna relented too, saying with an equal heaviness. 'If you can't find time to see me today, Sandro, then I'm afraid I *have* been wasting your valuable time. I did try to tell you that,' she couldn't resist adding, 'before you went off at half-cock.'

'Five o'clock,' he said. 'At the house.'

'No!' she instantly protested. 'I don't want to go there!' Then she bit her lip, knowing exactly how he was going to take that horrified reaction.

But his lovely house in Belgravia held only bad memories for her. She couldn't meet him there, would probably die of mortification before she'd even stepped over the threshold!

'Here, then,' he clipped. And now he really was angry: not hot, Italian angry but frozen, arctic angry. 'In an hour. It is all I can offer you. And don't be late,' he warned. 'I am working on a very tight schedule and as it is I will have to fit you in between two important meetings.'

'OK,' she agreed, wondering sinkingly if meeting him at his office was any better than meeting him at the house they had once used to share? In all honesty she had no idea, because she had never been to his place of work before. 'How—w-what do I do? When I arrive there, I m-mean?' she asked, her bottom lip beginning to feel as if it had been completely mutilated by her own anxious teeth. 'W-will I have to tell someone who I...? Only I don't like...'

'Coming out of hiding?' he suggested acidly. 'Or don't you like admitting your legal association to me?'

'Sandro...' she whispered huskily. 'Can't you appreciate how difficult I'm finding this to do?'

'And how difficult do you think I am finding it?' he threw back gruffly. 'You walked out of my life two years ago and have never bothered to so much as show your lovely face since!'

'You told me not to,' she reminded him. 'When I left, you said—'

'I know what I said!' he bit out. Then he sighed, and sighed again. 'Just be here, Joanna,' he concluded wearily. 'After all of this, just make sure you don't chicken out at the last minute and stand me up, or so help me, I'll— Oh, damn it,' he muttered, and the line went dead.

And suddenly Joanna *felt* dead: dead from the neck up, dead from the neck down. Dealing with Sandro had always ended up with her feeling like this. Drained, so sucked clean to the dregs of her reserves that it was all she could do to slump against the phone booth wall while she wondered wearily why she had set herself up for all of it in the first place!

Then a sudden vision of Arthur Bates sitting behind his cluttered desk as he issued his ultimatum flashed in front of her eyes, and, with the usual shudder, she remembered exactly why.

'Payment, Joanna, comes in cash or in kind,' he had

declared in that soft and silken voice of his. 'You know the score here.'

Payment in cash or in kind...

The very words had made her feel sick.

'How long have I got to pay?' she'd demanded with an icy composure that completely ignored the second option.

But the man himself had refused to ignore it. He had waited a long time to bring her down to this low point and he meant to savour every second of it. So he'd sat back in the creaky leather desk chair, inserted a heavily ringed finger into the gap between two gaping buttons on his overstretched shirt, then taken his time sliding his eyes over her slender figure, so perfectly defined beneath the tiny white waiter's jacket and black satin skirt she had to wear for work.

'Now would be good,' he'd suggested huskily. 'Now would be very good for me...'

Which had had the effect of freezing her up like a polar ice cap. 'I meant to pay the money.' She'd made it clear. 'How long?'

'A debt is a debt, sweetheart.' He'd smoothly dismissed the question. 'And you are already two weeks late with your payments.'

'Because I was off work with the 'flu,' she'd reminded him. 'Now I'm back at work I can pay you as soon as I—'

'You know the rules,' he'd cut in. 'You pay on time or else. I don't make them for fun, you know. You people come to me to help you out of your financial difficulties and I say, Yeah—good old Arthur will lend you the cash—so long as you understand that I don't take it nicely if you don't pay me back on time. It's for your own sake,' he contended. 'If I were to let you get behind, then you'd only end up in a worse mess trying to play catch-up again.'

He'd meant she'd have to borrow more from him to

keep up the extortionate repayments on his high interest loan and thereby sink further in his debt. It was a clever little ploy. One which kept him, the loan shark, firmly in control.

But for her it was different, and she'd always known it. Arthur Bates didn't want her money, he wanted her body, and by getting behind with her repayments she had played right into his hands. What made it worse was that she worked for him, which meant he knew exactly how much she earned; he knew he was in control of that part of her life. She waited on tables or worked behind the bar of his seedy little nightclub—the same club where she had got herself into debt by stupidly playing at its gaming tables.

Which actually meant that Arthur Bates believed he was in control of Joanna's life every which way he wanted to look at it.

But then, Arthur Bates didn't know about her marriage. He didn't know about her connection to the powerful Bonetti family. He didn't know she had a way out of the whole wretched mess—if she could find the will to use it.

Even with that will, she'd realized she was going to need time—time Arthur Bates was not predisposed to give her. So, there she had been, standing in front of him, feeling her skin crawl as his eyes roamed expressively over her, and she had done the only thing she could think of doing to gain herself time. She had lowered her lashes over the revulsion gleaming in her eyes, and offered him the sweet, sweet scent of her defeat.

'OK,' she'd muttered huskily. 'When?'

'You've finished for the night,' he'd said. 'We could be at my apartment in fifteen minutes...'

'I can't,' she'd replied. 'Not tonight, anyway...' And she had given an awkward little shrug of one slender white shoulder. 'Hormones,' she'd explained, and had hoped he was quick enough to get her meaning because she was loath to go into a deeper explanation.

He'd understood. The way his expression flashed with irritation told her as much. 'Women,' he'd muttered. Then, suspiciously, 'You could be lying,' he'd suggested. 'Using that excuse as a delaying tactic.'

Her chin had come up at that, blue, blue eyes fixing clearly on his. 'I don't lie,' she'd lied. 'It's the truth.'

'How long?' he'd asked.

'Three days,' she'd replied, deciding she could just about get away with that without causing more suspicion.

'Friday it is, then,' he'd agreed.

And she'd felt too sick to do more than nod her head in agreement before she'd turned and walked stiffly out of his office, only to slump weakly against the wall beside his closed door, in much the same way she was now slumping in reaction to Sandro.

Only there was a difference, a marked difference between having reacted as she had through sickened revulsion at what Arthur Bates *wanted* to do to her, and reacting like this through helpless despair at what Sandro *could* do to her.

Sighing heavily, she forced herself to move at last, pushing out of the telephone kiosk and hunching deeply into her thick leather bomber jacket as she walked the few hundred yards back down the street to her tenement flat in icy March winds—weather that grimly threatened rain later.

Letting herself into the tiny flat, she stood for a moment, heart and hands clenched, while she absorbed the empty silence that always greeted her now when she stepped inside. Then, after a small flexing of her narrow shoulders, she relaxed her hands, and her heart, and began removing her heavy jacket.

Time was getting on, making deep inroads into Sandro's one-hour deadline, yet, instead of hurrying to get herself ready for the dreaded interview, she found herself walking across the room to the old-fashioned sideboard where she stood, looking down at it as if it had the power to actually inflict pain on her.

Which it did, she acknowledged. Or one particular drawer did.

Taking a deep breath, she reached out and opened the drawer—that particular drawer.

And instantly all the memories came flying out; like Pandora's box, they escaped and began circling around her, cruel and taunting.

So cruel, it took every ounce of self-control she possessed to reach inside, search for and come out with what she had opened the drawer to find. Then she was sliding it shut again with a gasped whoosh of air from aching lungs, while clasped in her trembling hand was a tiny high-domed box that instantly spoke for itself.

Stamped on its base in fine gold lettering was the name of a world-famous jeweller—its provenance in a way, or a big hint, at least, that what nestled inside the box was likely to be very valuable.

But the contents meant far more than just money to Joanna. So much more, in fact, that she had never dared let herself lift the lid of the box in two long years.

Not since she'd glanced down one bleak miserable day and noticed her wedding and engagement rings still circling her finger and been horrified—appalled that she had walked out on her marriage still wearing them! So she'd scrambled around in her things until she'd found the box and had put the rings away, vowing to herself to send them back to Sandro one day.

But she had never quite been able to bring herself to do it. In fact, each time she'd let herself so much as think about Sandro, the old panic had erupted, a wild, helpless, anguished kind of panic that would threaten to tear her apart inside.

It had erupted in that telephone kiosk only a few

minutes ago. And it was doing it again now as she stood
here with the small ring box resting in her palm. Teeth
clenched, mouth set, grimly ignoring all the warnings,
she flicked open the box's delicately sprung lid—and felt
her heart drop like a stone to the clawing base of her
stomach.

For there they lay, nestling on a bed of purple satin.
One, a slender band of the finest gold, the other, so
lovely, so exquisite in its tasteful simplicity, that even
as she swallowed on the thickness of tears growing in
her throat her eyes could still appreciate beauty when
they gazed on the single white diamond set into plati-
num.

A token of love from Sandro.

'I love you,' he had declared as he'd given the engagement ring to her. It was that simple, that neat, that
special; like the simple, neat, special ring which, for all
of that, must have cost him a small fortune.

He'd given it to her with love and she'd accepted it
with love, she recalled, as the tears blurred out her vision
and a dark cloud of aching emptiness began to descend
all around her. For now their love was gone, and really,
so should the rings have gone with it.

She could sell them, she knew that, and easily pay off
her debt to Arthur Bates with the proceeds: just another
of the ways-out she had spent her sleepless night struggling with.

But she knew she couldn't do it. For selling these
rings would be tantamount to stealing from the one person in this world she had taken more than enough from
already.

She'd stolen his pride, his self-respect, and, perhaps
worst of all, his belief in himself as an acceptable member of the human race.

'You are tearing me apart—can you not see that? We
must resolve this, Joanna, for I cannot take much more!'

Those hard, tight words came lashing back at her after

two long miserable years and she winced, feeling his pain whip at her as harshly now as it had done then.

And it had been because of that pain that she had eventually done the only thing she could think to do. She had left him, walked out on their marriage to move in with her sister Molly, and had refused contact with Sandro on any level, in the hope that he would manage to put behind him the failure of their marriage and learn to be happy again.

Maybe he had found happiness, because after those first few months, when he had tried very hard to get her to change her mind and come back to him, there had been no more contact—not even when she'd phoned him up to tell him about Molly.

Molly...

A sigh broke from her, and, lifting her gaze from the box of rings, she glanced across the room to where a small framed photograph stood beneath the lamp on her bedside table and her sister Molly's pretty face smiled out at her.

Her heart gave a tug of aching grief as she went to drop down on the edge of her narrow bed. Gently laying the ring box aside, she picked up Molly's photograph instead.

'Oh, Molly,' she whispered. 'Am I doing the right thing by going to Sandro for help?'

There was no answer—how could there be? Molly was no longer here.

But Sandro was very much alive. Sandro, the man she had loved so spectacularly that she had been prepared to do anything to hang on to that love.

Anything.

But then, what woman wouldn't? Alessandro Bonetti had to be the most beautiful man Joanna had ever set eyes upon. The evening he had walked into the small Italian restaurant where she had been working waiting on tables had quite literally changed her whole life.

'*Alessandro!*' her boss Vito had called out in elated surprise.

She had glanced up from what she had been doing. Joanna could still remember smiling at the sight of the short and rotund Vito being engulfed in a typically Latin back-slapping embrace by a man of almost twice his own height.

Over the top of Vito's balding head, Sandro had caught her smile and had returned it as if he knew exactly what she was finding so amusing—which in turn had taken her laughing blue eyes flicking upwards to clash with the liquid brown richness of his.

And that had been it. Just like that. Their eyes had locked and an instant and very mutual magic had begun to spark in the current of air between them. His beautiful eyes had darkened, his smile had died, the full length of his long, lean fabulously clothed body had tensed up and his expression had changed to one of complete shock, as if he'd just been hit full in the face by something totally spellbinding. As she'd stood there, caught— trapped by the same heart-stopping sensations herself—she'd watched his hand move in a oddly sensual gesture across the back of Vito's shoulders, and, to her shock, had felt the flesh across her own shoulders tingle as if he had stroked her, not Vito.

'Who is this?' he'd demanded of the little restaurant owner.

Vito had turned towards Joanna and grinned, instantly aware of what was captivating his visitor. 'Ah,' he'd said, 'I see you have already spotted the speciality of the house. This is Joanna,' he'd announced, 'the fire outside my kitchen!' And both men's eyes had wandered over her bright hair, sparkling blue eyes and softly blushing face in pure Latin communion. 'Joanna—this is Alessandro Bonetti,' Vito had completed the introductions. 'My cousin's nephew and a man to beware of,' he'd warned. 'For he will be a dangerous match to your flame!'

A match to her flame... All three of them had laughed at the joke. But in reality it had been the truth. The absolute truth. Sandro lit her up like no other man had ever done. Inside, outside, she caught fire like dry tinder for him. And what was wonderful was the way that Sandro had caught fire with her.

It had been like a dream come true.

So what had happened to the dream? she asked herself as she sat there staring into space.

Life had happened, she answered her own grim question. Life had jumped out when she was least expecting it to steal the dream right away from her.

And overnight she had gone from being the lively, loving creature who had so thoroughly captivated the man she loved, into this—this—hollow wreck of a person who was sitting here right now.

A hollow wreck who was seriously about to place herself in Sandro's dynamic vicinity again?

Could she do it to herself?

Could she do it to him? That was the far more appropriate question.

Cash or kind.

Suddenly and without warning she began to shake—shake all over, shake badly. It had happened like this quite often since she'd had the 'flu.

But really she knew she was shaking like this because she had come full circle and back to making choices.

To making the choice that was no choice.

So she got up, put Molly's photograph back on the bedside table, walked over to the sideboard to replace the ring box in the drawer, then went grimly about the business of getting herself ready to meet with Sandro...

CHAPTER TWO

PRESENTING herself at Sandro's office premises at the appointed hour took every last ounce of courage Joanna had left in her—though at least she knew she looked OK. She had, in fact, taken great pains to make sure she looked her best—for his sake more than her own.

For Sandro was Italian; a sense of good taste, flair and style came as naturally to him as breathing. Joanna had witnessed him stroll around his home in nothing more than a pair of unironed white boxer shorts and a shrunken white tee shirt that showed more taut brown midriff than was actually decent—and still he'd managed to look breathtakingly stylish.

Then she grimaced, acknowledging that she had only seen him dressed like that once in their short but disastrous attempt at living together. Where most women would have found it a pleasurable experience to watch their men parade in front of them like that, she, on the other hand, had metamorphosed into a stone-cold pillar of paralysed horror.

Sexy? Oh, yes, he had looked sexy, with all of that dark, hair-sprinkled dusky brown skin on show, from long bare feet to strong muscular thighs, and his short, straight black hair looking slightly mussed, eyes sleepy because he had been dozing on the sofa, trying to combat the effects of jet lag because he had just flown back from a whistle-stop visit to his American interests. Even the signs that he needed a shave had not deflected from the fact that the man was, and always would be, sexy—to any woman.

Even this woman, whose only response had been to completely close down or go totally crazy.

Not that he had ever understood why she'd responded like that.

Not that she'd ever wanted him to understand why she'd reacted to his sexuality like that.

Yet, when she'd first met him, she had fallen in love with him on sight and had desired him so badly that sometimes she hadn't known how she was going to cope without them making love. But in those early days of their relationship he had been busy and she had been busy, and she'd also had Molly to think about.

They would wait, they'd decided. Until they were married, until she had moved in with him properly, when, at last, they would have time and space to immerse themselves in what was bubbling so hotly between them.

Then the unmentionable had happened. And it had all gone sour for them.

Her fault. Her fault.

How Sandro had put up with her like that for as long as he did would always amaze her.

Pain. That was all she had ever brought to Sandro. Pain and frustration and a terrible—terrible confusion that had finally begun to make his work suffer.

He was a banker by trade, a speculator who invested heavily in the belief in others. He was young, successful, a man with boundless self-confidence who'd had to believe in his own good judgement to have become the success he was.

Marrying her had affected that judgement, had corroded his belief in himself. Two bad investments in as many months had eventually finished him off. 'This cannot go on much longer,' he'd told her. 'You are stripping me of everything I need to survive.'

'I know,' she'd whispered tragically. 'And I'm sorry. So very sorry....'

Walking out of his life had actually been easy by the time they'd reached that stage in their so-called marriage. She'd done it for him, she'd done it for herself, and had found a kind of peace in the loss of all that terrible tension that had been their constant companion. A peace she hoped—knew—Sandro had found too. He must have done, because she'd seen his name in print over the past couple of years, in articles praising his unwavering ability to latch on to a good business investment when he saw one.

So, walking back like this was going to be hard in a lot of ways, not least because she sensed that a simple phone call from her had already set the old corrosion flowing through his blood. To Sandro she was like a virus, corrupting everything he needed to function as a normal and self-confident human being.

She would make this short and sweet, she told herself firmly as she set her feet moving through those plate glass doors behind which were housed the head offices of the Bonetti empire. She would explain what she wanted, get his answer, then get right back out of his life again before the corruption could really take hold.

And she would not show him up by presenting herself in faded old jeans and a battered leather jacket! So she was wearing her one and only decent outfit, which had escaped the clear-out she'd done just a year back, when anger, and grief, and a whole tumult of wild, bitter feelings, had made her throw out everything that had once had an association with Sandro.

Except this fine black wool suit cut to Dior's famously ageless design. The suit hung on her body a bit now, because she had lost so much weight during the last year or two, but most of that was hidden beneath the smart raincoat she'd had to hurriedly pull on because the threatened rain had decided to start falling by the time she'd left her flat again.

But, despite the raincoat, she felt elegant enough to

go through those doors without feeling too out of place, and she found herself standing in a surprisingly busy foyer, where she paused to glance around her, wondering anxiously what she was supposed to do next. Sandro hadn't answered her when she'd asked him that question; instead he'd got angry and slammed down the phone.

A sigh broke from her, tension etched into every slender bone, and her mind was too busy worrying about her next move to notice the way she caught more than one very appreciative male eye as she hovered there uncertainly, a tall, very slender creature with alabaster-smooth skin, sapphire-blue eyes and long, straight red-gold hair that shimmered like living fire in the overhead lights.

Beautiful? Of course she was beautiful. A man like Alessandro Bonetti would not have given her a second glance if she had not been so exquisitely beautiful that she turned heads wherever she went.

Not that Joanna was aware of her own beauty—she had *never* been aware of it. Even now, as Alessandro Bonetti stood by the bank of lifts across the foyer and witnessed the way half his male staff came to a complete standstill to admire her, he could see she was completely oblivious to the effect she was having on those men as her blue, blue gaze darted nervously about.

Nervous.

His mouth thinned, anger simmering beneath the surface of his own coolly composed stance. She'd never used to be nervous of anything. She might have lacked self-awareness, but she'd always glowed with vibrant self-confidence, had been strong, spirited enough to take on any situation. Now he watched her hover there like some wary exotic bird ready to take flight at the slightest sign of danger.

Her biggest danger, of course, being him.

She saw him then, and the fine hairs at the back of his neck began to stand on end in response to those eyes fixing on his own for the first time in two long years…

It was electrifying, an exact repeat of the first time their eyes had clashed across a room like this. Joanna felt the same charge shoot through her system like a lightning bolt. She stopped breathing, her heart seeming to swell so suddenly in her breast—like a flower bursting open to the first ray of sunlight it had encountered in so long—it was actually painful.

Why? Because she loved him—had always loved him. And knowing it quite literally tore her apart inside.

He was so tall, she observed helplessly. So lean and dark and sleek and special, with that added touch of arrogance he always carried with him, which only managed to increase the flower-burst taking place within her hungry breast.

He was wearing an Italian-cut dove-grey suit with a pale blue shirt and dark silk tie knotted neatly at his brown throat. His black-as-night hair was cut short at the back and styled to sweep elegantly away from his high, intelligent brow.

Her skin began to tingle, her eyes drifting downwards over sleepy brown eyes fringed by impossibly long eyelashes, and a thin, slightly hooked nose that was unapologetically Roman, like his noble bone structure, like his wonderful rich brown skin that sheened like satin over cheeks absolutely spare of any extra flesh.

And then there was his mouth, she noted with a dizzying swirl of senses that kept her completely held in their thrall. His mouth was the mouth of a born sensualist; it oozed sensuality, promised it, wanted and demanded it.

The mouth of a lover. The mouth of a Roman conqueror. The mouth she had once known so intimately that something inside her flared in burning recognition. It soared up from the very roots of her sexuality to arrive in a fire-burst of craving in her breast, making her gasp, making her own mouth quiver, making her want to taste that mouth again so badly that—

I can't do this! she decided on a sudden wave of wild panic. I can't be this close to him—face him like this and pretend to be cool and collected and indifferent to all of this—this excruciating attraction!

I've got to go. I've got to...

She was going to run, Sandro realised with a sudden tensing of his tingling spine. The urge to flee was literally pulsing in every tautly held muscle she possessed, and abruptly he jerked himself into movement, making her hesitate, bringing her flustered gaze fluttering up to clash with his own.

Where he locked it—with a sheer superiority of will; he used his eyes to lock her to the spot while he strode across the foyer towards her, as graceful as any supremely proficient cat mesmerising its prey before it pounced.

His movement brought the whole reception area to a complete and utter standstill, and the silence was stunning as all those present watched their revered employer make a bee-line for the beautiful stranger who had just stepped through their doors.

He reached her, pausing a careful foot away. 'Joanna,' he greeted quietly.

'Hello, Sandro,' she huskily replied, having to tilt her head back to keep looking into that very mesmeric face.

Then neither of them moved. For a long, timeless moment they simply stood there gazing at each other, enveloped by memories that were not all bad; some of them were, in fact, quite heart-wrenchingly wonderful.

So wonderful that her breasts heaved on a small, tight intake of air as a muscle deep down inside her abdomen writhed in recollection. Predictably she stiffened that disturbed muscle in rejection of her response.

Sandro saw and accurately read every single expression that flickered across her vulnerable face. The love still burning, the pain still hurting, the desire still clutching—then the inevitable rejection. His own eyes began to darken, sending back messages of an answering pain, of a desire that still burned inside him too and, perhaps most heart-wrenching of all, of a love well remembered, though long gone now.

After all—how could he still be in love with her after everything she had done to him?

He blinked then, slowly lowering and unfurling those impossibly long lashes as if he was using them to wipe away those answering messages and put in their place a cool implacability. Slowly his hand came towards her with the intention of taking her by the arm.

But Joanna saw the tendon running along his jawline tighten perceptibly as he did so, and was dismayed to realise that he was looking so tense because he expected her to flinch away from his touch in front of all these watching people.

She didn't flinch. Sandro couldn't know it, but she would rather die than show him up here of all places, on his own territory where he ruled supreme.

So his fingers closed around her elbow, and she felt the usual jolt of heat run along her arm in a direct warning to her brain that someone had invaded her personal space. But her blue eyes held his, calm and steady, and after a few more taut, telling moments, the tension eased out of his jawline and was replaced with a twist to his beautiful mouth that grimly mocked her small show of restraint—as if it offended him that she felt she had to protect his pride in front of all of these people.

'Come,' was all he said as he tightened his grip on her elbow then turned to begin drawing her across the silenced foyer, arrogantly ignoring every set of curious eyes that followed them.

'This is awful,' Joanna whispered self-consciously. 'Couldn't you have come up with a more discreet way of meeting me?'

'Discreet as in covert?' Sandro questioned drily. 'You are my wife, not my mistress,' he pointed out. 'My wife

I meet out in the open. With my mistress I am always very discreet.'

Stung to the core by the very idea of him being intimate with any woman, her heart began to fill with enough acid venom to curdle her system and blind her eyes to exactly where Sandro was leading her—until it was too late.

Then jealousy was suddenly being replaced by a crawling sense of horror that had her stopping dead in her tracks. 'No,' she protested huskily. 'Sandro, I can't—'

'Privacy, *cara.*' He cut right across whatever she had been going to say, 'is required before we begin.'

Privacy, Joanna repeated to herself, as the power of his grip forced her into movement again, propelling her into the waiting lift where at last he let go of her so he could turn his attention to the console.

The doors slid shut. They were suddenly alone. Alone inside a tiny eight-foot-square box with grey panelled walls and nowhere to run to if she required an escape.

No.

Her heart was in her mouth. As the lift began shooting them upwards her stomach shot the other way. It was awful. She closed her eyes, gritted her teeth and clenched her hands into two tight fists at her sides as an old clamouring reaction trapped her within a world of mindless dismay.

Sandro noticed—who wouldn't have noticed when she was standing there quivering with her teeth biting hard into her tense bottom lip? 'Stop it!' he snapped. 'I am not even touching you any longer!'

'Sorry,' she whispered, trying desperately hard to get a hold on herself. 'But it's not you. It's the lift.'

'The lift?' he repeated incredulously. 'Since when have your phobias added lifts to their great number?'

Sarcasm, she recognised, and supposed she deserved

it. 'Don't ask,' she half laughed, trying to make a joke of it.

But Sandro was clearly in no mood for humour. 'Another no-go subject I am banned from mentioning, I see.'

'Go to hell,' she breathed, her eyes squeezed tightly shut while she tried to fight off the soaring panic.

'And be virtually guaranteed to meet you there?' he derided. 'No chance.'

And once again they were sniping at each other. Like their telephone conversation earlier, they were proving yet again that they couldn't be in each other's company without all of this—emotion—spilling out.

The wrong kind of emotion.

'You may relax now,' he drawled with yet more sarcasm. 'We have come to a stop.'

Her eyes fluttered open to discover that they had indeed come to a stop without her even noticing it. The doors were open and Sandro was already strolling out onto a plush grey-carpeted corridor. He walked off, obviously expecting her to follow him. After having to peel herself away from the lift wall, she stepped out on decidedly shaky legs, feeling as if she were pulling a whole load of heavy old baggage along behind her.

He was waiting for her by a closed door, stiff-backed and angry. Smothering a heavy sigh, because this was all becoming so damned fraught—and she hadn't even got to the reason she had come here!—Joanna forced herself to walk towards him.

One of his long brown hands was resting on the door handle. He didn't so much as glance at her, yet still timed the moment he threw that door open so he instantly followed her into a big airy office where a very attractive blonde-haired woman of about Joanna's own age sat behind a desk.

She glanced up as they came in and smiled expectantly at them. But to Joanna's further discomfort Sandro ignored the look, not intending, it seemed, to introduce the two women.

And why should he? Joanna asked herself as she followed him across the room to another door. I won't be here long enough for it to mean much, even if he did!

When he opened the door he stepped aside again, obviously expecting Joanna to precede him. On an inner frisson of awareness to his electric closeness, she hurriedly brushed past him.

His office was a surprise—nothing like what she would have expected of the Sandro she used to know, she observed as she came to a halt in the middle of the room. This ultra-modern example of smoked grey executive decor bore no resemblance to the rich, dark wood antiquity of his private homes.

The door closed behind her. Joanna quelled the urge to stiffen up warily.

'Take off your coat,' Sandro coolly commanded.

Coat? She spun on her heel to stare at him, a fresh frisson of alarm stinging along her spine. She didn't want to remove her coat. She wasn't intending staying here long enough for it to be necessary!

'I—'

'The coat, Joanna,' he interrupted, and when she still didn't make a move to do it herself he began walking towards her, with his intent so clear that her fingers snapped up to begin undoing the buttons. He grimaced, mocking the fact that it took only the suggestion that he might try to touch her again for her to do exactly what he had told her to do.

Angry with herself for being so damned obvious, and annoyed with him for knowing her as well as he did, she drew off the coat and draped it across a nearby chair while he, thank goodness, diverted towards the big pale polished cedar desk standing in front of a huge plate glass window.

Then he turned and did the worst thing he could do

as far as she was concerned. He leaned his spare hips against the front of the desk, crossed his ankles, folded his arms across his wide chest, then proceeded to study her slowly, from her tensely curling toes, hidden inside plain black court shoes, to the top of her shining head.

She flushed, lowering her face and gripping tightly at the strap of her shoulder bag. He always did have this knack for completely discomposing her with a look, just as he was doing now—deliberately, she guessed. And she hated it. Hated what it made her feel inside.

But she had a suspicion that he knew that, too.

'You've lost weight,' he remarked finally. 'That suit hangs on you like an old sack. If you lose any more weight you will simply fade away. Why have you lost so much weight?' he demanded.

'I'm sorry,' she snapped. But surely he could work out *why* she had got so thin! It didn't take much knowledge of the last devastating year she had just lived through to understand it.

'Sorry—again, Joanna?' he mocked. 'I remember that being your favourite word before. It used to infuriate me then. It still does now,' he added grimly.

Her chin lifted, blue eyes flashing him a glinting warning that the very short fuse to her temper was alight. 'You said you were busy,' she reminded him curtly.

He dipped his dark head in wry acknowledgment of both the short fuse and the reminder that his time was precious. This was something else Sandro could never resist—riling her too-ready temper. He had once told her that it was the only really healthy emotion she had in her. He was probably right. It was the only one she had ever shown him during their short, disastrous marriage, anyway.

There was a knock at the office door. Joanna jumped nervously. Sandro grimaced at her nervousness, then his secretary was entering the room, carrying a tray set with coffee things.

The tension in the room must have been stingingly obvious, because she glanced warily at her employer, then skittered her gaze over Joanna, before murmuring some incoherent apology as she hurried across the room to place the tray down on a glass-topped coffee table set between two low leather sofas.

No one else moved. Sandro wouldn't, Joanna couldn't, and the silence gnawed in the air surrounding them all as the poor woman did what she had to do then turned to leave again with a brief, wary smile aimed somewhere between the two of them.

Joanna watched Sandro watch the intruder leave, watched him run his eyes over the woman from the top of her sleek blonde head to the slender heels of her black patent shoes. It was born in him to study women like that, Joanna was sure he wasn't even aware that he did it, but God she hated it!

Beautiful, she seethed in jealous silence. Of course the woman had to be beautiful! Sandro would not accept anything less in a woman who worked within such close confines!

'*Grazi*, Sonia,' he murmured rather belatedly, just as 'Sonia' was about to walk through the door.

She sent him a glance and it spoke volumes. Sonia was offended that he had not introduced her to his wife. But Joanna was only relieved. She had no wish to be nice to his secretary when she was too busy trying to subdue a second bout of jealousy that was so strong it literally fizzed beneath the surface of her skin.

Did Sonia do more than his typing for him? Could she be the very discreet mistress?

The door closed them in once again, and Sandro's attention was back on her. He studied her stiff-boned, firmly blank stance for a few moments, then sighed as though her very presence here irritated the hell out of him. He waved a long-suffering hand towards the seating area.

'Sit down for goodness' sake,' he muttered. 'Before your shaking legs give out on you.'

'They're not shaking,' she denied, but went to sit down anyway, choosing one of the sofas and perching herself on the very edge, hoping he wouldn't play his old trick of sitting himself down beside her. It was just another tactic he'd used to employ to completely unsettle her. He'd used to gain some kind of morbid gratification from placing her on the defensive.

But this time, she was relieved to see, he decided not to bother with that one. Instead he turned his attention to pouring out two cups of coffee.

Joanna watched his every move, every deft flick of those long brown fingers as he poured out two black coffees, added sugar to his own but none to hers, used the small silver spoon to stir the sugar, then silently handed a delicate white china cup and saucer to her, before going to sit down on the sofa opposite with his own.

And he did it all without bothering to ask her if that was how she liked her coffee. Sandro possessed almost instant total recall. He could remember names, places, facts and figures without having to try very hard. It was a major asset in his line of business, he had once told her, to possess fast recall of any information he might have acquired concerning the subject under consideration at the time. It saved him a lot of hassle because it meant he didn't need to waste time going off to gather up the information.

On top of that, he was astute, *very* astute. Few people managed to con him. Though she was one of those few who had managed to do it. And in some ways she believed he'd found that harder to forgive than anything else she had done to him.

'OK,' he said flatly. 'Let's have it.'

She shook, rattling the delicate bone china cup in its

saucer so badly she had to lean forward and put them down before she spilled the coffee all over herself.

Sandro crossed one elegant knee over the other. That was all, no other reaction whatsoever, but the action captured her restive attention. He was wearing charcoal-coloured socks, she noticed inconsequently. His shoes were hand-made lace-ups in a shining black leather.

'I need some money,' she mumbled, hating herself for having to ask him, of all people, for it.

'How much?'

Just like that. No hint of surprise, no raised voice. She had never asked him for anything before, not even a tube of toothpaste. He knew that. The man with total recall would remember that telling little fact.

Which also meant he had already worked out that this was a dire situation for her.

'F-five...' The rest got stuck in her tension-locked throat and she had to swallow before she could say it. 'Five thousand pounds.'

Still nothing. No reaction whatsoever. She even glanced up, wary, puzzled, searching his impassive face for a hint of what he was thinking.

She saw nothing.

'That is a lot of money for you, Joanna,' was the only comment he made.

'I know,' she admitted. 'I'm s...' Sorry, she had been going to say, but she stopped herself and instead got stiffly to her feet, unable to remain still beneath that dark level stare for a single moment longer.

With a tight restlessness she moved herself away from his close proximity, aware that his eyes were following her, aware that his brain was working faster than any other brain she had ever known.

Aware that he was waiting for her to tell him what she wanted the money for but was determined not to ask her himself.

Reaching his desk, she rested the flat of her hips

against its edge and crossed her arms over her body so her icy fingers could curl tensely around her slender arms.

The silence between them began to stretch; she could feel it vibrating like a tautened wire between them. But, in a way, it made her want to do something to stop it, so she turned abruptly to face him, lifted her chin and forced herself to look directly into his carefully neutral eyes.

'I have a proposition to put to you,' she announced. 'I need some m-money and, since you are the only person I know who has any, I thought you could give it me in the f-form of a settlement.'

'A settlement to what?'

Her heart suddenly decided to stammer. 'A divorce.'

No response, not even a flicker of those long, lush, lazy lashes, the super-controlled bastard!

'I know you can't possibly want to hang onto this so-called marriage of ours,' she raced on quickly. 'So I thought it might be best to make a clean break of it.'

'For five thousand pounds?'

Her cheeks warmed with guilty colour. 'Yes.'

'So, let me get this straight,' he recounted, 'You want to divorce a multi-millionaire for the princely sum of five thousand pounds. Now that, Joanna, insults my ego,' he informed her, moving at last to get rid of his own cup and saucer, then relaxing back again. 'Why not go for the jackpot and demand half of everything I own?' he suggested. 'After all, you are entitled to it.'

No, she wasn't. She wasn't entitled to anything from Sandro, not even the five thousand she was asking him for. 'I just want f-five thousand pounds,' she reiterated, staring down at some unremarkable spot on the smooth grey carpet, because the next bit was going to be even harder to say, and she couldn't look at him while she said it. 'And I need it today, if you can lay your hands on that much.'

'Cash?'

She swallowed, then nodded. 'Please...'

No reply. Again she was forced to look up so she could search his face for a hint of what he was thinking—and she saw nothing but a sudden terrible gravity that almost cut her in two.

Face flushing, she dropped her gaze once more, agitated fingers picking at the fine woollen sleeves of her suit jacket.

'Perhaps you had better tell me why you need it,' Sandro suggested very quietly.

'I've got myself into debt,' she admitted, so softly that Sandro was lucky to hear it. 'And the people I borrowed the m-money from are riding my back for payment.'

He heard. 'Who?' he demanded. 'Who exactly is riding you?'

She didn't answer, her small chin lowering to her chest in an act of sinking shame, and another tense silence followed because she found that now she had come this far she just didn't have it in her to tell him the full truth. He was bound to be so disappointed in her!

She had never done anything a man like Sandro would consider worthy. It had used to annoy him that she worked at two different jobs as a waitress, six days and nights out of seven each week. He could never understand why she had no ambition to do something better with her life. He'd disliked the tiny flat she used to share with Molly, and had even offered to put them both up in something more fitting.

But more fitting for whom? She'd always suspected he'd meant fitting for a man like him to visit; that, in his own way, Sandro was ashamed of his little waitress girlfriend, even if he was too besotted at the time to walk away from her.

And, on top of all of that, he hated gamblers. Said they were weak-willed losers in life who wanted everything the easy way. How did you tell a man who thought like that that you'd spent the last year working in a casino for miserable peanuts, only to gamble those peanuts away at the tables yourself!

She couldn't. It was as simple as that. She could not do it. And she was just wondering if he would detect a lie if she came up with one that would cover a five-thousand-pound debt, when he pulled one of his other little tricks and confused her by suddenly changing the subject.

'Where have you been living recently?' he asked.

'Here in London.' She shrugged.

'Still waiting hand and foot on other people?'

'Yes.'

He sighed, his disappointment in her clear this time. 'You did not have to go back to doing that kind of job, Joanna,' he said grimly. 'When we parted, I had no intention of leaving you so destitute that you had to return to that.'

'You owed me nothing.' And both of them knew there was more truth in that than really bore thinking about.

'You are my wife!' he bit out raspingly. 'Of course I owed you something!'

Which led them neatly back to the money, Joanna wryly supposed.

'What I find difficult to believe,' he continued, 'is that you, of all people, have got yourself into that kind of debt entirely on your own! In fact,' he extended frowningly, 'you always shied right away from the risk of getting yourself into debt for even the smallest amount.'

She grimaced, shamed and contrarily mollified by those few words of praise from this, her biggest critic. He was right, money had never been one of her gods—not in the shape of cold, hard cash in the pocket, that was.

'So, who is it for, Joanna?' Sandro demanded grimly. 'Who really needs this five thousand pounds you are asking me for?'

Her chin came up, the frown puckering her smooth brow telling him that she did not follow his meaning. 'It's for me,' she stated. 'I got into this mess all by myself.'

But he was already shaking his head, expression grave again, saddened almost. 'It's for Molly,' he decided. 'It has to be. Has your sister managed to get herself into financial difficulties, Joanna?' he demanded. 'Is that what this is really about?'

Whatever Sandro had expected her to do or say at this very critical point, he certainly had not expected her to draw the air into her body in the short, sharp way she did—or for her face to drain of every last vestige of colour.

'My God, that was cruel,' she breathed out eventually, staring at him as if he had just thrust a ten-inch blade into her chest. 'How could Molly be in trouble,' she choked out thickly, 'when you already know she is dead?'

CHAPTER THREE

SANDRO'S reaction was to shoot to his feet. 'What did you say?' he raked out hoarsely. Then, 'Please say again,' he commanded, sounding as though he had suddenly lost his grasp of the English language. 'For I think I must have misheard you.'

'But you knew!' Joanna cried. 'M-Molly was knocked down and killed in a traffic accident twelve months ago!'

'No!' The angry denial literally exploded from him. 'I do not believe you!'

But Joanna wasn't impressed. 'I rang you—right here, at this office!' she contended. 'You wouldn't speak to me, s-so I left a message with your secretary!'

That secretary? she wondered suddenly. Had she spoken with the lovely Sonia that day her whole world fell apart?

'You rang here?' What she was saying was finally beginning to sink in. He sounded punch drunk, suddenly looked it too—utterly punch drunk. 'Molly is dead?'

'Do you honestly think I would lie about something like that?'

Of course she wouldn't, and acknowledgement of that fact actually rocked him right back on his heels, shock ripping down the full length of his lean, tight body as he stood there and stared at her—stared while his richly tanned face went pale.

Then, quite without warning, the famous Bonetti self-control completely deserted him and, on an act of savage impulse, he spun jerkily on his heel and brought his clenched fist crashing down on the glass-topped table!

Joanna gasped, eyes widening in numb disbelief as delicate china rattled on impact, then began to bounce upwards, tumbling through the air to land with a splintering crash just about everywhere! The glass table-top broke, not splintering like the china, but folding in on itself and shattering into big lethal pieces.

The ensuing silence was appalling. Broken china and glass, spilled sugar, cream and coffee lay spread across everything—the two grey leather sofas and the carpet!

And there was Sandro. Sandro slowly straightening from the utter carnage he had just wreaked, teeth bared, lips tightly drawn back, face ashen, blood oozing from the knuckles of his still clenched fist.

'Oh, no,' she whispered, coming out of her horrified daze to push a trembling hand up to mouth. 'You didn't know...'

'Astute,' he clipped, driving his uninjured hand into his pocket to come out with a clean handkerchief.

He began wrapping the handkerchief around his bloody knuckles while, shaken to her very roots, all Joanna could do was stand there and watch him. She tried to breathe but found that she couldn't. Her lungs seemed to have seized up while her heart was thundering against a steel casing of shock that had wrapped itself tightly around her chest.

The door suddenly flew open, Sonia almost falling into the room with it. 'Oh, good grief!' she gasped, her eyes going wide in horror as they took in the carnage.

'Get out!' Sandro barked at her, swinging a look of such unholy savagery on her that she whimpered with a muffled choke and quickly stepped out of the room again, shutting the door behind her.

'Th-there was no need to take your anger out on your secretary,' Joanna murmured in tremulous reproach.

Sandro disregarded the rebuke. 'I never got your message,' he bit out. 'Did you think I would have ignored it if I had? You did,' he realised, seeing the answer etched into her unguarded face.

She had insulted him. Simply allowing herself to believe that he didn't care about Molly's death was probably the biggest insult she had ever given him.

And she had given him a few, Joanna acknowledged. 'I'm...'

'Don't dare say it,' he warned her gratingly.

Her mouth snapped shut, then on a shaky little sigh it opened again. 'At first I refused to believe you would just ignore her death like that,' she allowed. 'But when I heard nothing from you, f-for days and days, I decided you...' An awkward shrug finished what really no longer needed to be said. 'And I was in shock,' she continued huskily. 'I could barely think straight. It was only after the f-funeral, w-when I'd moved from the flat and found somewhere else to live because I couldn't bear to stay there without—without...' She couldn't say Molly's name either, 'It was only then that it really began to sink in that you hadn't—hadn't...'

At last she stumbled into silence. Sandro didn't say a word, not a single word, but just ran his uninjured hand across the top of his sleek dark head, dropped it stiffly to his side again, then turned away from her as if looking at her at all offended him.

'I'm sorry' hovered on the tip of her tongue again but managed to stay there while she simply stared at him, feeling helpless, feeling guilty, feeling hopelessly inadequate to deal with the fractured emotions clamouring around the two of them.

'When?' he asked suddenly. 'When did this happen?'

She told him the date, her low-pitched voice unsteady.

'Madre di dio,' Sandro breathed.

Molly had been killed a year ago to the very day.

Then he was moving, making her eyes instantly wary as he strode towards her, right past her, to angrily round his desk. His hand snaked out, catching up the telephone, while his other hand remained tensely at his side, the handkerchief bandage slowly staining red.

'I want a print-out of all calls to this office on this date a year ago,' he snapped at whoever was on the other end of the line. 'And while you are about it you will bring in last year's appointments diary.' Slam. The telephone landed back on its rest.

Joanna blinked, still staring, still stunned by the incredible display of emotional fury from this man who was usually so controlled. It was awful, she *felt* awful for being the one to cause it. And it only got worse because, quite suddenly, he dropped into the chair behind his desk then slumped forward, both hands going up to cover his face.

Once again the desire to say sorry was hovering precariously close to the edge of being spoken. She had truly believed that he was no longer interested in anything that happened to her. It had caused her so much hurt at the time—oh, not only because of her own wretched feelings of desertion, but also for Molly. Molly, who had thought the world of Sandro.

Joanna had hurt him with her bitter and twisted view of everything life had to throw at her. Now she wanted to go to that desk and put her arms around him, hold him—offer him some kind of consolation for the shock she had just dealt him.

But she couldn't because her own maimed senses wouldn't let her. So she turned and moved away a step or two, then just stood with her arms tightly folded across her body and her eyes grimly lowered from the temptation of Sandro, who looked still so in need of comfort.

The tentative knock which came on the office door before it hesitantly opened was actually a relief.

Sandro straightened in his seat, face still pale, features drawn, eyes so black they wrenched at Joanna's useless heart strings.

He didn't look at Joanna but honed his attention directly onto his secretary. 'The print-out you asked for,' she murmured, hurrying forward to place it down on the desk in front of him. 'And last year's appointments diary...'

Sandro began scanning the print-out while Sonia hovered warily, uncertain what was expected of her—she was curious, curious enough to keep sending Joanna furtive glances that scurried away before their eyes could clash.

'I was away in Rome throughout the whole month of March,' Sandro sighed out eventually.

Sonia nodded. 'I remember,' she said, and heat bloomed into her cheeks.

Guilty heat? Knowing heat? I-remember-because-we-were-there-as-lovers kind of heat? Jealousy licked a sandpaper-rough stroke along Joanna's backbone, stiffening it, leaving it tight and tingling.

'So, who took over here?' Sandro demanded.

'Luca brought his own secretary here with him,' Sonia explained, then dared to ask the big question. 'Why? Was there some kind of oversight?'

'Oversight?' Grimly Sandro repeated the word and let loose a short huff of a laugh. 'You could say that,' he clipped out, then, heavily, 'OK, Sonia you can leave this with me now.'

A dismissal in anyone's books. If they were lovers, Sandro obviously knew how to keep the two relationships separate.

'Discretion' was the word he had used himself.

Sonia walked stiffly out of the room, leaving another fraught silence in her wake. 'Come here, Joanna,' Sandro commanded grimly.

But that awful, blinding, bitter jealousy was now licking its way around her whole body and she couldn't move a single muscle. Didn't dare even glance at him, because if she did she would be spitting out filthy accusations, like, You're sleeping with that woman while you're still married to me, you bastard!

'Joanna...'

Oh, God, why had she come here? Why had she set herself up for all this grief? Grabbing desperately at some hint of composure, she walked forward until once more the flat of her hips touched the desk.

'Read,' he commanded, stabbing a long finger at a single line of type on the paper print-out.

It was a list of some kind. Frowning, she leaned a little closer so she focused on what was written. 'Female asking for Mr Bonetti,' it said. 'No name. No message.'

'This is a computer print-out of all telephone calls that come into this suite of offices,' he explained. 'Look at the date. Look at the time. That was you calling me, wasn't it?' he suggested gently. 'On the day of Molly's accident you called here, and in your shock and confusion when you could not get through to me personally you forgot to leave your name or mark the urgency of why you were calling, didn't you?'

Had she? Was that what she had done? She frowned, trying to remember, but found that she couldn't. That dreadful day was very hazy. She could barely remember anything about it except trying to contact Sandro.

'And see this...' he continued levelly, turning the old appointments diary to face her next. The whole of the month of March was scored through with a pen. 'ROME' it had printed in big letters. 'I was not in the country. I was, in fact, away for the whole month.'

'You don't have to go to these extremes to convince me it was an oversight,' she murmured uncomfortably. 'I believe you without it.'

'Thank you,' he said.

'You're not a liar,' she tagged on with a jerky shrug of one slender shoulder. 'Your honesty and integrity have never been in question for me,' she felt constrained to add.

'Well, thank you for that, also,' he very drily replied.

Then in one of those quick-fire changes of mood he could undergo which tended to make her flounder, he suddenly stood up and rounded the desk.

'Come on,' he said, taking a grip on one of her hands.

She stiffened up like a board, but he ignored the stiffening, being so used to it from years ago. Just as he had become used to having to ignore it if he wanted to go on touching her. He began pulling her towards the door.

'But where are we going?' she demanded warily.

'My hand needs attention,' he clipped out, that was all.

The door opened, he pulled her through it, then pulled her past his wide-eyed, beautiful secretary without so much as glancing her way, out of that office, down the corridor and into a waiting lift.

Another damn lift.

He let go of her at the one time in her life when she wished he'd hang on tightly, digging his unwrapped hand into his inside jacket pocket and coming out with what looked like a plastic credit card. Sliding the card into a narrow slot in the lift console, he pressed one of the floor buttons, then slid the card out again.

But Joanna didn't see which floor number they were going to; she was too busy bracing herself for the moment when those wretched doors would close them in.

'You are quite pathetic, do you know that?' he observed deridingly.

Yes, she acknowledged, she knew it, but knowing it didn't stop the war of abominable memories she was desperately trying to suppress.

The doors closed, the lift began moving, and she pressed herself back against its panelled wall, expecting to begin sinking downwards—but didn't. The lift shot up, then came to an almost immediate stop again.

Startled, she opened her eyes to find Sandro watching her with a half-frowning, half-contemptuous expression.

She stared back, vulnerable—without knowing it, she looked vulnerable.

The doors slid apart. Sandro wrenched his gaze away from her and walked out of the lift, like the last time, obviously expecting her to follow him.

She did so reluctantly, once again having to peel herself away from the wall and walk forward on shaking legs—only to stop dead two steps on to stare bewilderedly around her.

'Where are we?' she asked sharply.

'Up one floor,' Sandro replied. 'In my private apartment, to be exact.'

Predictably, all hell broke loose inside her, blue eyes flickering around her new surroundings like a trapped animal looking for a means of escape. 'Y-your apartment?' she repeated unsteadily. 'Here?'

'Yes,' he confirmed, his tone spiked. 'Convenient, is it not?'

He knew what she was thinking. He knew what she was feeling. He knew that to her, a private apartment meant intimacy, and intimacy translated into panic.

She flicked him a very wary glance. He answered it with a mocking one, challenging her to protest, to give in to what was beginning to bubble up inside her and run screaming for the dubious safety of the lift behind her.

A choice of two evils. Like the one she'd had to make between facing Sandro again, or facing what Arthur Bates had in store for her.

Then there was no choice to be made, because the lift doors gave a soft warning whoosh. She almost jumped out of her skin, spinning jerkily around to stare as her one means of escape smoothly closed on her.

'Well, well,' Sandro drawled so silkily she winced. 'Caught like a frightened little mouse in a trap. Poor Joanna. But please,' he continued before she could retaliate against his biting sarcasm, 'make yourself at home, if you can,' He was dry and he was cutting. 'I need to attend to my injured hand.'

Then he had gone, disappearing through a door and leaving her hovering there, staring dazedly around her.

It was nice, was the first sensible thought to reach through the scramble her mind had become. The lift had opened directly into a large airy sitting-room that reflected Sandro's very classical Italian tastes much more than his ultra-modern office had done.

Pale pastel-shaded walls made a tasteful backcloth to timeless pieces of elegant antique furniture that blended easily with the more modern oatmeal sofas and easy chairs sitting comfortably on a thick-piled cappuccino-coloured carpet.

No smoked glass to pound his fist into here, she noted wryly—only to feel her breath catch in her throat when she relived the appalling sight of Sandro, of all people, losing control of himself like that. It just wasn't like him. Sandro had always been the most patient and controlled person she knew.

He had to be, around you, a small voice inside her own head grimly taunted. She sighed, the dark, weighty truth of that sitting heavily on her narrow shoulders.

Then he was back without warning, striding through the door he had disappeared through a few minutes earlier, and instantly any feelings of guilt or remorse she might have been experiencing towards him left, because she was suddenly feeling that inner sun-burst of pleasure begin to erupt all over again, holding her captive; she was mesmerised by the sheer animal sexuality of the man.

His jacket had gone, and his tie; the top button to his pale blue shirt had been yanked impatiently open at his taut brown throat, the sleeves rolled up his hair-peppered arms.

'Here,' he said. 'Do this for me.'

She blinked, trying to clear the hypnotic effect he was

having on her, her darkened eyes lowering to the snowy white towel he now held to his injured hand.

'It needs covering until it stops bleeding,' he explained, holding out a band of sticking plaster to her.

But he was much too close, much too vibrantly, aggressively, electrifyingly real. So real she could feel his body heat, could smell the subtle tangy scent of him. Her fingers fluttered, her nails scraping against the sides of her skirt, lungs beginning to fill her chest as memories swam up from the depths of nowhere, memories of how it had felt to be held against his warm, tight, very masculine body. And she wanted him. She closed her eyes, almost groaned out loud. How badly she wanted to feel this man against her, around her, deep, deep inside her!

'Joanna!' His voice was tight, it was angry, and it showed how completely he misunderstood the reason why she was standing here white-faced and quivering like this. 'I am asking you to place a small plaster on my hand—not take all your damned clothes off!' Offence shuddered through him on a wave of personal resentment that stiffened his muscles and hardened his face. 'I will do it myself!' he raked at her harshly.

'No!' she protested, her emotions hitting an all-time high of helpless confusion 'No,' she repeated huskily. 'I'll do it.'

Quickly she took the dressing from him, plucking it with a snap from his fingers and ripping away its protective paper casing.

In hot, acid silence, he let her remove the covering towel and inspect the damage, her trembling fingertips carefully checking for tiny shards of glass while her teeth clamped hard into her tense bottom lip because his eyes were boring into the top of her bent head with such bitter antipathy.

'Can you feel anything in that?' she asked, pressing gently either side of the open cut.

'No.'

'It isn't as bad as it could have been,' she remarked, as casually as she could. 'It was a stupid thing to do, Sandro.'

'Believing me capable of ignoring your sister's death was stupid.'

Joanna grimaced. It was true, and she had been stupid. Stupid with shock, stupid with grief, stupid in so many ways that at this precise moment she didn't dare let herself think about most of them.

'So, tell me how it happened,' he requested quietly.

Her fingers stilled in the act of smoothing the plaster across his grazed knuckle, then, almost unknowingly, they straightened, stretching out along the length of his. Only Sandro's fingers were longer than her own, stronger, but beautifully sculptured, the short nails well kept and neatly rounded, his skin warm to the touch.

'She was on her way to college,' she murmured in a voice devoid of emotion. 'Standing at the bus stop when a car ploughed into her. Its breaks had failed,' she explained. 'The driver lost control... Molly wasn't the only one to be killed outright,' she said flatly. 'Three more people died and another three were seriously injured. It was in all the newspapers at the time,' she added huskily. 'Names printed. Addresses...' Which was why she had been so sure that Sandro had to have heard what had happened. Even if he'd missed her phone call, he couldn't have possibly missed the press coverage.

And quite suddenly she began to shake with those wretched violent spasms that had been catching her out when she least needed them. Sandro muttered something in Italian and the next thing Joanna knew she was being folded against him and held there fast by determined arms.

'Weep on me if you want to,' he invited thickly. 'You never know, I may even join you!'

A joke? No, he wasn't joking; the situation was just too wretched to turn into a joke. But she didn't weep.

She hadn't wept in years, couldn't weep—wouldn't weep.

Why? Because she knew that if she so much as gave in to the smallest sob, then the floodgates would open wide and the whole lot would come pouring out.

Everything—everything.

So instead she just stood there, letting him hold her, gaining some small measure of comfort from his all-encompassing embrace. But she needed to cry—she knew that, in some deep, dark place in her; she knew she was teetering right on the very edge of a complete mental collapse if she didn't release some of the monsters lurking inside her.

'I am sorry I wasn't here for you, *cara*,' he murmured.

'It doesn't matter now,' she mumbled into his warm brown throat.

It was the wrong thing to say, obviously, because he was suddenly angry again. 'Of course it damned well matters!' he rasped, pulling away from her to leave her standing alone, feeling cold and deserted, having to fight a desperate urge to throw herself against him again. 'You make a cry to me for help for the first time ever—and I do not answer you!' His sigh was harsh as he abruptly spun his back towards her. 'Of course it bloody well matters,' he repeated gruffly.

And here I am, thought Joanna, one year later, and making another cry for help. Only this time it's money I want, not commiseration.

No comparison.

Which also brought her neatly back to the reason why she was here at all.

Money. The one commodity which Sandro had in abundance, and in which she had never shown the slightest interest before. In fact, how they'd ever got to the stage of wanting to marry each other was a real enigma to her. She'd lived in a cheap bedsit and waited on other people for a living. Sandro's homes were all in the very best places. His London townhouse was in Belgravia, for instance, and his elegant Italian apartment a mere stone's throw away from Rome's Colosseum.

Even this penthouse, this small-by-comparison apartment that she hadn't known existed until today, was something out of the ordinary to a girl like her. But a handy apartment situated above his place of business was a reflection of the man's wealthy lifestyle.

In short, Sandro came from top-drawer Italian stock and had never waited on another person in his life. He lived surrounded by luxury, he travelled in luxury, he *wore* luxury like a mantle that demonstrated his exclusivity.

Yet what had happened to this very exclusive man? He'd taken one look at the little waitress in a tiny backstreet Italian restaurant, and had seemed to fall flat on his very exclusive face for her.

She'd never understood it. But had never thought to question it because she'd been so young then, so innocent and naïve and eager to fall in love and *be* loved by this man who, to her besotted eyes, had been a god among men.

And he'd treated her with such tender loving care— wooed her in the old-fashioned way, with flowers and small presents and gentle kisses that had not been allowed to get out of hand even though they'd both known it was frustrating the hell out of both of them.

'I want to marry you with respect. I want you to come to me wearing the white of a virgin and to know I am paying the correct price for the gift of that virginity.'

Oh, dear God, she thought painfully now. Beautiful words, warm and caring—enchantingly romantic words. Words that had given him idol status in her impressionable mind.

But it had been those same beautiful words that had finally ruined it all for them.

Would always ruin any hope they had of being anything but poison to each other.

Suddenly he spun back to face her. Their eyes caught, and she wondered if his own thoughts had been taking him down similar painful pathways because he looked so damned sad.

'Did she feel anything?' he asked. 'Was she in any pain before she——?'

He meant Molly. He had been thinking about her sweet-natured baby sister, not herself. She shook her head. 'It was instant, so they tell me. She would not have known much about it.'

'Good.' He nodded. Then, out of the dull, throbbing silence that powered down around both of them, a telephone began ringing somewhere in the room.

Sandro muttered something and strode off to answer it. '*Si?*' he bit into the receiver—a sure sign that he still had not got himself totally in hand yet, because he had spoken in his native tongue.

He listened, his dark eyes snapping with irritation. 'No—no,' he said. 'You must cancel. I am too involved here.'

Cancel? Cancel what? Joanna wondered, then, on a jolt of understanding, 'Oh—no, Sandro!' she protested. 'Please don't cancel your meetings on my account!'

But he was already replacing the receiver on its rest and turning back to her with an expression carved into his features that had her old friend panic skittering to life.

He looked like a man who had come to a decision, and that decision most definitely involved her. 'Sit down,' he invited, 'while I pour us both a drink.'

'But y-you told me this morning that you were very busy,' she reminded him anxiously. 'And—and I have to be leaving now anyway!' she lied as her eyes darted over to the closed lift doors, as if they could be her saviours and not the source of one of her worst nightmares.

'Leave without your five thousand pounds safely stashed away, *cara*?' he mocked. 'What a waste of all this anguish you have been putting yourself through by making yourself come to me.'

And it was absolutely amazing—Joanna made incredulous note. Today Sandro had swung himself through just about every emotion that existed. Now he had come full circle and was back to being the sharp-eyed cool headed businessman again, while she—

Well, she was back to making choices, seeing Arthur Bates' grotesque figure looming threateningly in front of her and knowing that once again she had to draw the same conclusion she had drawn each time she reached this same unpalatable point.

There was no choice.

She was caught, held fast in a trap of her own making. Her own fears, failures and wretched inadequacies the bait with which she had ensnared herself.

As if knowing all of this quite instinctively, Sandro turned away from her pale-faced defeated stance and moved over to a cupboard which, when opened, revealed a comprehensive selection of bottles and glasses.

No choice. Those two little words began to rattle with dizzying speed around her head until she had to give in to them and sit herself down—before she actually fell down. She chose one of the soft oatmeal linen-covered chairs, dropping into it and lifting a shaky hand to her aching eyes; that lingering 'flu virus, worry and lack of sleep were really beginning to get to her.

On top of all that, she mocked herself grimly, there was all the stress entailed in making herself come here; it was no wonder she was feeling drained to the very dregs of her reserves now.

The cold touch of glass against the back of her raised hand brought it jerking away from her eyes.

'Try this,' Sandro advised. He was standing over her, holding out a glass. 'Gin and tonic,' he informed her as she stared suspiciously at the contents. 'It may help give you back some courage. You seem to be flagging.'

Mock, mock, mock. She took the glass, put it to her lips and swallowed half its contents down in one go in sheer defiance.

He ignored her defiance, going to seat himself in the chair opposite to sip more slowly at his own drink, looking supremely relaxed while her body was bone-gratingly stiff, his eyes annoyingly implacable while hers were giving much too much away.

'Since when have you had this apartment up here?' she asked, cowardly, shying away from what she knew she should be talking about—the money.

'Since always,' he replied. 'It has always been here.'

She frowned. 'But I never knew about it.'

'That is because I have a perfectly acceptable house in Belgravia where I preferred to live with my *wife*,' he answered with sardonic bite. 'This place is merely a convenience for when I have to work late. Time zones being the inconvenient things they are,' he explained while her own mind leapt backwards and began wondering if all those nights when he hadn't come home to the house in Belgravia while she'd lived there he had been right here instead.

The perfect escape from the pressure of his lousy marriage.

'Where are you living now, exactly?' he asked casually, bringing her mind crashing back into sharp focus on him.

But she had to look away from him as she answered that question, not wanting to see the distasteful expression that was bound to cross his face.

It was clear in his voice, though; she could not escape that. 'Do I have to presume, from that kind of address, that the five thousand pounds is protection money?'

Inside she shuddered. Sometimes, she decided, she hated him—despised his sarcasm and his superior attitude. 'I can protect myself!' she snapped.

He made no comment—a derisory comment in itself. She took another deep slug at the gin and felt her head start to swim. She'd had no food today, couldn't remember when she'd eaten last, so the alcohol was hitting her empty stomach and instantly entering her bloodstream.

'All you have to do, Joanna, is say it,' Sandro suggested gently.

'Say what?' Her eyes flashed him a wary glance.

'Say what you need the money for and I will give it to you.'

Just like that? No strings attached? She could barely believe her luck—except for one small thing. It was confessing *why* she needed the money that was the most difficult.

'I've been working behind the bar in a casino nightclub for the last twelve months,' she said, trying to sound casual and knowing she failed dismally. 'S-since Molly died,' she added, because it was in actual fact a very important part of why she was here today. 'I...' Her glass was empty and she was suddenly wishing it wasn't.

'A refill?' Sandro offered, getting smoothly to his feet.

'Please.' She held the glass out to him. He took it and walked away, giving her a few moments to sag while he wouldn't see her doing it.

'So,' he prompted as he mixed her second gin. 'Molly died and you went to work in a casino. What happened next to make the penny-conscious Joanna get herself into debt?'

Did he know—had he guessed? She frowned at his back and couldn't decide. He was acute, he was perceptive, he always had been able to out-think her brain ten to one in any discussion. But...?

No, she decided, even Sandro wouldn't suspect her, of all people, of gambling.

Gambling. The word on its own could actually make her feel physically sick now! Or was it the gin? Or the lack of food? Or the stress she had been living under recently?

Or was it just sheer reluctance to confess the full truth that was making her feel so sick?

He came back, handed her the refilled glass. She accepted it and took a gulp at it while he returned to his own chair.

'Please go on,' he invited.

'When—when Molly died, I...' Fell apart, was the wretched truth of it. She'd felt as if she had nothing and no one left to live for. 'The job was offered to me by the same man who lent me the money to pay for Molly's funeral...'

The choking sound coming from Sandro brought her eyes up to clash with his. He wasn't quite in focus, she realised—which made it easier to keep this story moving.

'He said I could pay him off quicker if I worked for him,' she explained. 'B-because the wages were higher than restaurant work, and he could even find me a flat within walking distance of the club. S-save me travelling expenses...'

'But it turned out to be not as simple as that?' Sandro grimly suggested.

She gave a shake of her bright head. 'H-he kept on putting up the weekly repayments, and I suppose I st-started to panic in case I fell behind, which therefore m-meant borrowing more money from him. I'd seen some of the other girls get caught out like that,' she explained huskily. 'It was f-frightening...'

'So, you did what?' Sandro demanded. 'To keep up your payments?'

Joanna took another gulp at her gin as if her very life depended on it. 'I played the tables,' she confessed on a soul-crushing rush of shame. 'I took a chance on trying to win back what I owed him. It didn't work.' Well, who in this room is surprised at that? she wondered grimly. 'One—one thing led to another,' she went on. 'And now I'm in debt so deep to him that if you won't help me, then...'

She trailed to a stop, aware that she had said too much already.

But Sandro wasn't going to let her stop there. 'Then...?' he prompted.

She shrugged, refusing to answer, and lifted unfocused eyes to him. 'Will you help me?' she asked.

But even through a gin-induced haze, she could see the anger in Sandro's expression. 'I want to know what happens if you do *not* pay this man off!' he grimly insisted.

And her own temper flared, putting a bright, condemning spark into her blue eyes as she tossed at him bitterly, 'Oh, you should know the answer to that one, Sandro, since you once used very similar tactics on me yourself, in an effort to get me to do what you wanted me to do!'

'What the hell is that supposed to mean?' he demanded.

'Blackmail!' she flashed at him, and uttered a scornful little laugh. 'Which is probably the most polite way of describing the pressure you exerted to get me over the colossal hurdle of—now, what did you call it?' She pretended to ponder, angrily ignoring the slow, warning way his body was stiffening in the chair opposite. 'Ah, I remember. My "freakish aversion to sex!" That was it! Only where you used your wonderful self as a lever, this man is using my debt to get what he wants from me!'

CHAPTER FOUR

'I NEVER used force on you!' Sandro denied that.

But, 'Let me make love to you or get out of my life', had been force enough, Joanna argued silently. In the end, when she still could not let him touch her, she had saved him the bother of throwing her out and walked out on him instead!

'So let me get this straight,' he continued angrily. 'What you are trying to say here is that some man is forcing you to have sex with him in return for the five thousand pounds you owe to him?'

'Yes!' That was exactly what she was saying!

Then, quite without any prior warning, she was getting rid of her glass and lurching to her feet, turning away from Sandro and hugging herself, a hand pressed against her quivering mouth.

He was slower in rising, his anger replaced by a grim kind of recognition of what it was she was struggling with. He had been here before after all—had seen it all before.

After a few moments of watching her, he released a heavy sigh. 'OK, Joanna,' he murmured quietly. 'Take it easy. No one is going to touch you like that here.'

Her bright head nodded in acknowledgement of his grim reassurance. 'I'm sorry,' she breathed behind her straining hand, and for once Sandro did not chide her for the apology.

All he did do was move right away from her, going to stand by the window, staring out, giving her some privacy while she pulled herself together again.

Yet for some reason that small show of sensitivity hurt

her so badly it sent the wretched tears sweeping across her eyes. She didn't understand it, couldn't explain it, but it had something to do with the man himself and the way he was standing there, tall, sleek, unbearably special, hands resting in the pockets of his grey silk trousers, shoulders straight, that noble dark head held high.

And he was alone.

That was what hurt. It was the space between them, the huge gulf, physical and emotional. A gulf she had caused and one he maintained because he had learned the hard way not to attempt to bridge it.

And what had she just done? Thrown into his face one of those very few times he had attempted to cross that wretched bridge.

Dropping her hand to her side, she clenched it into a tight fist of bitter aching despair. It wasn't fair—none of it. They'd had so much going for them once, and now look at them.

Miserable, both of them. Each better off without the other.

He turned half towards her, giving her hungry senses a view of his long, lean shape in profile. 'If I give you the money, what then?' he asked.

'I'll pay off the debt,' she said.

She couldn't offer to pay Sandro back because it would take her years to save up that kind of money on a waitress's meagre pay. Which was why she was offering him a divorce as compensation.

'And you'll stop working for him?'

'Of course,' she declared, as if that should be obvious. 'I never want to set eyes on him or his nightclub again, if I can help it.'

'And the gambling,' he persisted, despite that statement. 'Does that stop also?'

'Of course,' she repeated, almost affrontedly this time. She was not going to fall into the same trap again in this lifetime; did he think she was a complete fool?

'There is no "of course" about it,' he sighed. 'Gambling is a disease, and you know it. If you can use it as an excuse to get you out of financial difficulties once, you are likely to use it again if the situation ever presents itself. Then what comes next?' He turned to fully face her, his expression so stone-cold serious that she shivered. 'Do you have to force yourself to come to me again, and will I be expected to pay up again, and keep on paying until you do what you are really trying to do to yourself, Joanna? Tip yourself head-long into the deep, dark pit you struggle so hard to stay out of?'

He knew about the pit? Her whole body jolted with horrified shock. Sandro knew about the big black hole she spent most of her waking hours staring into, watching it open wider and wider with each passing day...

'You are refusing to help me?' she breathed in a frail little voice that seemed to absolutely infuriate him.

'Damn it, Joanna! I am not refusing you!' he exploded in frustration. 'But I would be a fool if I did not insist on some assurance from you that this will not happen again!'

'It will never happen again,' she promised instantly.

But it wasn't enough. She could see it wasn't enough. The way his lips clamped together and his hand raked through his hair told her he was not content with just her verbal promise.

Fear struck a direct line down her trembling spine, the sudden thick silence that fell between them locking up her throat as she stood there staring at him in an open plea, while he frowned darkly down at his feet.

Then he gave a sigh, sounding like a man who was surrendering to something he had no wish to surrender to. 'Give me the name of the club and the name of the man,' he clipped out.

'Why?' she questioned warily. 'W-what are you going to do?'

He didn't reply, but his eyes, when they lifted up to

clash with hers, sent a fresh wave of dread run[?]
through her. He didn't trust her to deal with this problem
properly, so he was going to deal with it himself! He
was going to go to the nightclub, would see the kind of
place she worked in, see the kind of man she had stupidly got herself embroiled with. And his opinion of her
was going to hit rock bottom—if it wasn't already floun-
dering near there already.

'Come on, Joanna,' he prompted very grimly. 'You
say you have no wish to see this—person or his place
of business again. So, prove it,' he challenged. 'Give me
all the relevant information and I will deal with it for
you.' And when she still stood there, saying nothing, he
added very softly. 'Or you don't get a single penny from
me.'

Her heart split open, surrender spilling out from the
jagged crack—along with the hapless knowledge that
she had nowhere else to turn if she refused his wretched
offer. And she gave him the information in a breathless
rush of words that turned his face to granite as he recognised names and places where the lowest of the low
lurked.

Weak-kneed by it all, she dropped back into the nearest chair as Sandro strode grimly by her, eyes hard,
mouth tight, his whole demeanour one of utter bone-
clenching distaste.

And why not? she asked herself miserably. She felt
the exact same way about it all herself!

A shaky hand fluttered up to touch her brow. She
really should not have drunk all that gin, she realised,
because now, on top of everything else, her head was
beginning to throb.

'Luca?' Sandro's hard voice cracked like a whip over
the top of her bowed head. She looked up to find him
holding the telephone to his ear again. 'Get five thousand
pounds out of the safe and meet me in the foyer with
it,' he commanded. 'And I want two of our security men

standing by with the company limo. What?' he snapped, his frown as black as thunder. 'No, not for protection! For damned intimidation!'

Joanna winced. Tight-lipped, Sandro turned abruptly and walked over to a door which, she presumed, led through to the rest of the apartment. He disappeared through it without so much as glancing her way; that was a further condemnation, just another thing she had been judged on and found utterly wanting.

He came back looking so different from the man who had left the room five minutes before that Joanna shot to her feet, and then just stood there staring, trapped into a sense-sizzling silence by the whole incredible transformation.

He had changed his clothes. Gone were the dove-grey trousers and the pale blue shirt with its casually open neck and rolled up sleeves. In their place he was wearing a very dark pin-striped three-piece suit made of the kind of fine fabric that shrieked money at her from every superbly-stitched invisible seam. A pristine white shirt sat neatly around his brown throat, knotted with a slender red silk tie.

But none of that—devastatingly effective power-dressing as it was—caused her breath to catch and her eyes to widen in horrified appreciation of what he was out to achieve by dressing himself like this.

It was the full-length black cashmere overcoat he had slung about his elegant shoulders that made the real statement, along with the fine black wool scarf hanging negligently along his lapels and the stretch-tight black leather gloves he was tugging over his long fingers.

Sandro was a man on a mission. A man aiming to make an immediate impact before he even opened his tight-lipped mouth. Every inch of him screamed Italian, from the arrogant way he had slicked back his jet-black hair to the unblemished shine on his black leather shoes.

He also screamed power. He screamed danger.

'W-what are you going to do?' she asked breathlessly.

At first he didn't answer, his lean face closed up as tight as a drum, eyes as hard as iron, mouth like steel, so deeply sunk into his chosen persona that her heart began to quail in her trembling breast.

'Pay your debt for you,' he clipped out.

Pay the debt or kill the lender? she found herself extending nervously, and almost laughed—not with amusement, but in sheer nervous response to the strange kind of sensual arousal that was suddenly tugging at the lining in her abdomen. The whole thing—Sandro, how he looked and what she was experiencing because of that look—was disturbing her in ways she could barely cope with.

'You—you're not going there to start trouble are you, Sandro?' she questioned cautiously. 'He—he has bouncers with him all the time. Big guys who don't mind h-hitting instead of listening.'

'And you are concerned that I cannot take care of myself?' It was mockery, hard and spiked.

Her tongue ran an unsteady track around her paper-dry lips as she sent her gaze skittering over that lean tight body locked inside those beautiful clothes.

'Th-they'll eat you for breakfast,' she told him flatly.

He laughed, not in the least disturbed by her opinion. 'They will not lay a single finger on me, *cara*, be sure of it.'

Because he was taking this man Luca with him, and two of his security guards? He must be mad or just plain arrogant if he truly believed that.

'I'm coming with you.' At least she knew these people, was even on friendly terms with some of them. They would listen to her before using their fists. But with Sandro in this mood, in *this* frighteningly provoking guise... She shuddered, glancing distractedly around the room for her bag, only to remember annoyingly that she had left it with her coat downstairs in Sandro's office. 'I left my bag and coat in your...'

'You will remain right here.'

Voice soft, dripping ice; that was all he needed to say to bring her scrambling mind into full focus. Spinning back to face him, Joanna found those iron-hard eyes fixed on her for the first time since he'd entered the room, and suddenly the tension sizzling between them was enough to fill her with a spine-tingling sense of dread.

'Sandro—please don't do this!' she pleaded, wringing her hands in front of her. 'I know these people! I can deal with them. I don't want you to be hurt!' she concluded shrilly.

He didn't bother to deign to give all of that a reply, but simply strode to the lift, tapped the call button with a leather-coated finger, watched the doors slide obediently open, then stepped firmly inside.

The doors closed. Joanna stood there staring at them, feeling angry and frustrated and useless and wretched—so damned wretched that her eyes filled with hot aching tears.

He was gone for over two hours, and in that time she worried herself into a nervous frazzle. She paced the floor. She tried out each chair, only to find she couldn't sit still in any of them. She even found the will to face the horrors of a lift journey, after a sudden decision to go and collect her bag from downstairs and then go after him.

But when she pressed the lift call button nothing happened. The ruthless swine must have disabled it so it could not leave here!

By the time he reappeared she was locked into a state of brittle high anxiety, sitting in a chair, shoes off, knees tucked up beneath her chin, arms hugging them tightly.

But her knees dropped and her spine straightened as her anxious eyes quickly checked him over from the top of his slick-styled head to the tips of his shining shoes. The overcoat had gone, the gloves and scarf, but there was no sign of any physical damage, she noted with a sinking sense of relief. No cuts or bruises, except the ones on his fist he had caused to himself earlier.

'Your receipt,' he drawled, dropping a flimsy scrap of paper down on her lap.

He moved away immediately, going over to the drinks cabinet where he helped himself to what looked like a neat whisky.

Helplessly her eyes lingered on him, then slowly dropped to the piece of paper. 'Joanna Preston,' it said. '£5,000 paid in full.' And Arthur Bates' signature was scrawled beneath.

'You don't even use my surname,' Sandro remarked, his back to her.

She didn't use his name because she had never felt she'd earned the right to use it, but to say that out loud was the surest way to bring other, much more unpalatable subjects lurking out into the open. So she kept her eyes lowered, bit down into her tremulous bottom lip and said nothing.

He turned, glass in hand, then simply stood there looking at her for what seemed like an age, until she couldn't stand it any longer and glanced up warily. 'Thank you for this,' she said, fingers fluttering across the receipt.

He made no comment; there was no expression in those lean dark smoothly sculptured features. She knew he was angry, knew he felt like spitting nails at someone—preferably her, she ruefully accepted. But for some reason he was keeping it all firmly dampened down inside him.

'That place was the pits,' he said.

Not *that* dampened down, she noted, and she flushed, looking quickly away from him again.

'At least when you waited in a restaurant there was some dignity to it,' he went on grimly. 'But that place was an insult to yourself, Joanna. Why did you go there?'

She shrugged and refused to answer. What was the use? He wouldn't understand it if she tried to explain it to him. After all, what did a man like Alessandro Bonetti know about having nothing, or being nothing, either to yourself or to others.

He could stand there in his smart suit of clothes, that most probably had cost twice as much as the five-thousand-pound debt he had just discharged for her, looking down his classical Roman nose at her, as if the insult she'd given herself had also rubbed off on him. If that was the case, then he should be grateful that she had *not* used the Bonetti name!

'Well, that side of your life is now over,' he suddenly decreed. 'So we will not speak of it again.'

Subject closed. Joanna lifted her head to stare at him, refusing to believe what she was really hearing—what she had a horrible feeling she was hearing threaded between the actual spoken words.

'I'm not going to live with you again, Sandro,' she said, coming stiffly to her feet.

'No?' he challenged, and folded his elegant arms across his equally elegant chest. 'Then where are you going to live?' he enquired, so smoothly that she sensed the trap even as she walked herself right into it.

'I still have my flat,' she declared. 'I will find myself another job easily enough!'

He didn't say a damned single word, but Joanna knew, even as he then unfolded his arms and began walking towards her, that her world was about to come tumbling down right into Sandro's waiting clutches.

Dipping a hand into his jacket pocket, he slid it out again so smoothly that she almost missed the fact that he had collected something as he moved. Then she saw it, and sure enough, everything came clattering down on top of her.

She fell back into the chair, her eyes fixed and staring. 'W-where did you get that?' she gasped.

'Where do you think?' he drawled, and dropped the tiny photo frame onto her lap before moving away again, leaving her to stare down at her sister's sweetly smiling face and come to terms in her own time with what it meant for him to be in possession of it.

'I have stored most of your things at the house in Belgravia,' he continued quite casually. 'But I did bring a few essentials back here with me...'

Lifting her shock-darkened eyes, she watched him stroll into the lift, only to come out again almost instantly. He was carrying a suitcase—one of her own suitcases, she recognised—which he stood against the wall. Then he smoothly straightened.

'Y-you've been in my flat!' She gasped out the obvious.

He nodded. 'Been in it, been appalled by it. Been so damned angry as I stood there in the middle of it, seeing how my wife—*my wife*!' he repeated angrily, 'was living! Here...' Striding back to her, he calmly added her bag to the growing stack of possessions he seemed hell-bent on piling on her.

And each one sent its own message, she realised mutely. The receipt for the money, which told her she was now in his debt. Molly's picture frame taken from her bedside table, which told her he had been to her flat. Now her bag, which was telling her exactly how he had found and gained access to the flat in the first place.

And don't forget the suitcase, she told herself grimly. Your own suitcase, personally packed by this man, which is telling you clearly that he has gone through all your personal things like a robber!

'I can't believe you've actually done this!' she choked out shakily.

'Done it,' he confirmed, 'and finished it,' he added. 'There is not a loose end left to be tied as far as I can tell. Your flat has been emptied, your lease has been closed, your job terminated and your debts paid. Did I miss anything?' he enquired with an acid innocence that did not hide the burning antagonism beneath the surface of his calm demeanour. 'Ah, yes,' he drawled, bringing those elegantly clad legs in her direction while all she could do was sit there and look at him, too totally, mind-numbingly stunned to do much more than blankly watch his approach.

Coming to lean right over her, he braced his hands on the arms of her chair so she was quite effectively pinned where she sat.

'There is you,' he said, eyes hard, expression tight. In fact, he was so locked into his role of macho intimidator that he didn't even seem to care that he was seriously frightening her. 'You, *Signora Bonetti*,' he murmured, using the name like a dire threat, 'are about to begin the first day of your new life.'

'I don't know w-what you think you are talking about,' she stammered, shifting nervously back in the chair as his face came ever closer.

'No?' he quizzed. 'Then let me explain it to you. Because this is the deal, *cara*. No bartering, no haggling. I have paid your five-thousand-pound debt for you. I have sorted out your life for you. And in return you, my dear *wife*, are going to start being a *wife* to me!'

'I can't believe you're even saying this!' she spat into his determined face. 'It makes you no better than Arthur Bates—can't you see that?'

She shouldn't have said that, she accepted warily, when she saw the kind of sneer that tugged an ugly line into his beautifully moulded mouth. 'Oh, surely I am the much better option, *cara*,' he contended softly. 'Even you, with your distorted view of the whole male race in general, must be able to appreciate that!'

Appreciate it? Of course she could appreciate it! Did he think she was blind as well as stupid? But appreci-

ating what Sandro undoubtedly was by comparison
every other man she'd known—never mind the awful
Arthur Bates!—did not alter the fact that she could not
let him do this to her. Could not let him do it to himself.

Not again. She shuddered. Never again.

'I hate you,' she whispered, her voice shaking on the
wicked lie. 'You can't possibly want to live with a
woman who can't so much as stand you touching her!'

That should have sent him into recoil—she had said
it to make him do exactly that. But Sandro seemed to
have some hidden agenda of his own here, because instead of recoiling, to her consternation he laughed.

'Hate?' he mocked. 'Can't stand me touching you?
You have been hungrily eating me up with your eyes
ever since you set foot into my building!' he accused.

'That's a lie!' she denied.

'A lie?' His hard mouth curved upwards, without actually smiling. 'Well, let us just see, shall we?'

And, with no more warning than that, he took hold of
her arms and pulled her to her feet as panic came back
to envelop her. She hit out at him with her closed fists,
imprisoned arms struggling to break free from his grasp.

'So wild,' he muttered, fielding her blows by capturing her wrists and using them to pull her hard up against
him. 'So very wild when protecting that precious virtue
you hang onto so tenaciously!'

Her mind went white—a complete white wipe-out of
bright, blinding pain that had her fighting all the harder
to get free. Pulling, pushing, kicking, scratching. 'Let me
go!' she choked, trying uselessly to twist her captured
wrists free.

'Never,' he declared. 'You are back with me now.
And this time I will make sure you stay!'

Then his dark head was lowering, his parted mouth
angling across her own tensely held lips, his arms coming around her, imprisoning her, holding her trapped by
the one thing she feared the most.

The power of his kiss.

It was like being tossed back through dark lonely chasms to a time when she'd barely existed between moments like this.

Sandro—Sandro—filling her mind, her heart, her body with a wild, wanton need that broke through every single barrier she had ever erected between them. It was wonderful, it was right, it was like touching Heaven after spending years as an outcast in Hell. It was heat after the big freeze; it was solid land after being cast adrift. It was her destiny rediscovered in the soul-healing crush of his warm, wonderful mouth.

She groaned, whimpering because she could feel herself coming alive, every emotion she possessed exploding through the constraints she exerted over them. Her lips began to cling instead of trying to break free, her heart was thundering with a power that almost completely enveloped her, breasts tightening, their tips seeming to waken from a long, long sleep that now set them pulsing and stretching, reaching out like twin sensors towards the only stimulus that ever roused them.

And deep, deep down inside her a fire began to erupt, an old fire, a fierce fire, a fire that was lit only by the match this man had the power to strike.

He felt it. His mouth lifted from hers, his parted lips moist and pulsing. 'Cara mia...' he breathed, bringing her stunned blue gaze jerking up to meet the driven blackness of his. 'I knew it.'

'No,' she denied, trying—trying to tug it all back under wraps again.

But it was already too late. She could see it burning in the knowing glitter of his darkened eyes, see it in the flush of heat striking out from his high cheekbones, could feel it in his body that was slowly tightening with desire against her.

She could taste it in his mouth, which was suddenly

covering her own again with a passion that left her no room whatsoever to scurry back into hiding.

Sandro had kissed her before many times. He had kissed her gently, he had kissed her coaxingly, he had even kissed her teasingly—especially during those earlier, happier days of their relationship. Later had come the impassioned kisses, the ones he'd struggled to keep in check because their desires had ignited so easily then. After they were married, and frustration began to play a vital part in any kisses they used to share, he would kiss her hungrily, sometimes angrily, but mostly with a painful kind of plea that used to tear her apart inside.

But this was different. This wasn't teasing, or angry, or anything like that wretched pleading that used to tear her apart so much. This was mutual need, pure and simple, and it flooded through both of them in a hot and torrid gush of dark, dizzying pleasure.

Then, 'No,' she breathed. 'I can't do this.' And she abruptly broke free of him, taking a couple of very necessary steps backwards, haunted eyes fixed on his oddly sombre expression, considering the victory he had just won over her defences.

'Why can't you?' he asked, very, very gently.

Tears washed across her eyes, then left again. 'I can't,' she repeated shakily—then, almost tragically, *'I just can't!'*

He sighed, a flicker of pain disturbing his long, lush lashes—before he was grimly blanking it out. 'None the less,' he said firmly, 'this is where we begin, *cara*, not where we end it. Now, come,' he commanded, giving her no chance to clear her brain of one trauma before he was resolutely swinging her into another by firmly taking hold of one her hands.

Ignoring the way she tried to break free from him, he pulled her towards the waiting lift. 'We are late,' he informed her as they reached it. 'We will have to hurry if we are to make it in time.'

'But—where are we going?' she demanded, trying not to react to a new wave of panic, which belonged to the lift, not to Sandro's grimly determined behaviour as he pulled her inside it.

'You will see soon enough,' he replied, holding onto her wrist as he turned to set the lift doors closing.

Then his attention was fully back on her, his grip shifting to her slender waist as he propped her up against the lift wall and held her there. They began to move. She closed her eyes and tried very hard to fight the whole gamut of horrors suddenly rocketing through her. Not least was his closeness, the shattering residue of that incredible kiss they had just shared, and his words, which had carried such a threatening thread of finality with them.

And, of course, there was the lift, that wretched lift.

'Tell me, why are you so frightened of travelling in this lift?' Sandro asked huskily.

She shook her bright head, eyes squeezed tight shut, face white, trembling lips pinned back against her clenched teeth.

'I can feel your heart fluttering like a trapped butterfly...'

And you're too close and I can't breathe, and I feel like I'm about to explode with stress! she thought hectically.

He kissed each of her pulsing temples, brushed his mouth over each quivering eyelid before doing the same thing to either corner of her quivering mouth.

'Don't...' she breathed, turning her head to one side in rejection, then, contrarily, her hands were jerking up from her sides and clutching tightly at his jacket lapels in case she drove him away.

It was awful, this dizzying tumble of confused emotions that wanted their own safe space—yet they wanted him to fill it. She wasn't even sure if she was reacting like this because of the lift or because of Sandro any more!

'You are so very beautiful—do you know that?' he murmured with an excruciating low-voiced intimacy. 'Even after all of these years, you can still take my breath away.'

'I'm poison for you,' she gritted, hating him—loving him.

'You don't taste like poison,' he said, and ran the moist tip of his tongue along her extended jawline. 'You taste of vanilla. I adore vanilla...'

Oh, dear God! 'Sandro!' she pleaded. 'I can't bear this!'

'Me or the lift?' he questioned huskily.

'Both!' she cried. 'Damn it—both!'

'Well, the lift has stopped moving,' he informed her lazily. 'Which only leaves me to wonder why you are still clinging to me as though your very life depends on my being this close to you...'

Stopped? Her eyes flicked open, struck directly into his—his smiling, mocking, teasing eyes, eyes that were challenging her even as they darkened with yet another message that had her fingers flexing on his jacket lapels.

'No,' she protested.

'Most definitely,' he insisted. Then he kissed her again, long and deep and achingly gently.

'This is it, Joanna,' he warned as he drew away again to watch her lashes flutter upwards to reveal eyes dazed by a hopeless passion. 'So keep looking at me,' he urged. 'For this is what I am now. Not the guy who crept stealthily around your problems the way I did the last time we were together—but this man. The one who means to invade your defensive space at every opportunity he gets. And do you know why?' he enquired of those dazed and shimmering pure blue eyes. 'Because each time I do it, you shudder with horror less, and quiver with pleasure more. An interesting point, don't you think?'

Was it? She didn't think so; she thought it was utterly terrifying. What was happening to her? Had the two years of never letting herself go near him made her so hungry, so desperate, that she couldn't even fight herself any more?

'I can never be a proper wife to you,' she warned him, and she meant it—knew it as a fact so solid that even this dreadful, aching clutch of need would never change that for her.

'You think so?' he pondered. Then, 'Well, we shall see.'

At last he moved away from her, gave her space to wilt, then pull herself together, gave her the chance to take in her strange new surroundings.

They seemed to have arrived in a basement car park, judging by the rows of cars she could see beyond the lift's open doors. One, in particular, stood like a shiny black statement of wealth right in front of them: a long and shining luxury limousine.

Sandro took a grip on her arm again and led the way towards it. A man dressed in a black chauffeur's uniform jumped to open the car's rear door. Sandro saw Joanna inside, then followed her, and it was only as she shuffled quickly along the soft leather seat in an effort to place as much distance between them as she possibly could that her fingers made contact with something soft and bulky. She glanced down to find Sandro's black overcoat, scarf and gloves lying tossed on the seat like yet another statement.

The war guise of a man on a mission, she recalled, and shivered. Because it was becoming very clear that Sandro was still on that mission. Arthur Bates had only been one part he had already dealt with; the rest of Sandro's mission involved herself.

'Where are we going?' she dared to ask, once the car

was in motion and sweeping smoothly out into thin
March daylight.

He didn't answer immediately, so she sat there tense,
waiting with her senses already prepared for him to say,
The house in Belgravia.

But he didn't. Instead his hand went into his jacket
pocket and came out with something else to drop casually onto her lap. 'You forgot to put these on when you
came out this morning,' he drawled. 'Put them on now.'

It was her ring box. Her fingers fluttered down to
touch it. Her ring box which had been safely stashed
away inside her drawer of memories when she'd left her
flat this morning.

Her drawer of memories, which Sandro must have
sifted through. He must have seen what was hidden
there. Her wedding photograph, in which she stood in
her gown of flowing white silk beside this man, dressed
not unlike the way in which he was dressed right now.
A photograph that wasn't framed like Molly's picture
because it was just too painful to be placed out on show,
so it had gone in the drawer with her other painful me-
mentos.

Wild colour ran up her throat and into her cheeks in
a mottled flush of mortification. She stared at the box,
just kept staring fixedly at it while Sandro stared at her
bent head, knowing.

It was crucifying, knowing that he now knew how she
had kept every tiny insignificant thing he had ever given
to her. The simple but exquisitely made gold studs for
her ears and the fine link gold bracelet with its double
heart safety catch. The pretty lace-edged handkerchiefs
embroidered with her name and never used because he'd
had them made specially during one of his trips abroad
and she treasured them too much. Or the stack of post-
cards, one for every journey he had taken away from her
in those months leading up to their wedding day. 'Missing you' was all he had written on every one, but—her

throat locked—'Missing you' had meant so very, very much.

Then there was the silly set of toy cartoon characters, one for each quickly snatched lunch they had shared between his busy working day and her lunch and evening shifts at a fast-food restaurant. But of all those none of them bruised her heart more than the knowledge that Sandro had looked into the very private and personal centre of her, and had seen the leather-bound book, inside which was lovingly pressed the head of a flower from each bouquet he had ever given her.

Hot tears stung across her eyes, then were winked away again. She couldn't speak, didn't even try to. Sandro let the knowing silence pulse between them for a while, then reached out with a long gentle set of fingers to her chin, pushing it upwards so she had no choice but to look directly at him.

'They are safe,' he assured her. 'You need not worry.'

The tears came again, and again were winked away, but not before he'd seen them, and not before she had witnessed the expression written in his.

'Sandro...' she began unsteadily.

But—no. He was not going to allow her to say anything he did not wish to hear right now.

'We are going to Heathrow.' He totally threw her by announcing this, letting go of her chin, letting go of her eyes, and returning to man-on-a-mission mode again. 'We catch the late afternoon flight for Rome, where we will begin from the very beginning again.'

From the beginning.

Joanna sat there, stunned into total paralysis as the full meaning of those coolly delivered words sank in. Rome, where they had begun their married life three years ago. Rome, where it had all gone so terribly sour for them. Rome, to his beautiful apartment overlooking the Colosseum.

Rome. They were going back to Rome, to begin at

the beginning again. Only this time Sandro intended to make sure the outcome was nothing like the last time. She knew that without him having to say so out loud. Knew it because every single thing he had said and done since he arrived back from seeing Arthur Bates had told her as much.

'I can't do this...' she whispered.

'Put on your rings,' was all he replied.

CHAPTER FIVE

THEY flew out from London's cold grey skies into the warm blue of the Mediterranean. Joanna barely noticed. She barely spoke, barely focused on anything going on around her. She felt emotionally grid-locked, trapped, with no way to turn, nor any hope of escaping from the coils of control Sandro had smoothly bound about her.

He had done it all within a few short hours of leaving her locked away in his plush penthouse prison. Not a bad achievement, she grudgingly acknowledged. He had dealt with Arthur Bates, gone directly to her flat to clear it out, terminated her lease, made their arrangements to fly to Rome, then returned to deal with her.

Efficient? She'd always known him to be efficient. Stubborn? It went without saying that a man of his character must be stubborn or he would not be so effective. Determined? No question about it; the very foundation of his success in life was built on his own steadfast determination to succeed.

But suicidal? She could not bring herself to believe that he was crazy enough to want to set himself up for a second dose of married life with her.

But every time she opened her mouth in an attempt to reason with him he seemed to sense the words coming, and he would reach across the gap between their two seats to pick up her hand and raise it lazily to his lips, where he would keep it, his breath warm against her trembling skin, while he continued reading the business papers he had brought with him on the trip and waited patiently for her to subside again.

Only when she eventually subsided did he let her have

her hand back. The man was unassailable when he had his mind set on something, and, right now that something was his failed marriage, and his estranged wife who had been foolish enough to go to him in her hour of need.

Now she rued that decision more than she had ever rued anything else in her entire life—except marrying him in the first place, of course.

'Sandro…' She actually managed to get his name out before her took hold of her hand.

'Not now,' he said, his attention still fixed on his precious papers. 'I like privacy when I fight with you, *cara*. Try to contain yourself until we reach home.'

Home. A short sigh broke from her and she twisted her hand free from his so she could subside again, her eyes bleak, her concerns acting like spurs to her agitated nerve-ends—which were not allowed to appear agitated because Sandro did not like public scenes.

And she adhered to that because—despite every bitter and resentful thing she was feeling—she still, still could not bring herself to show him up in public.

But his Rome apartment would always be the place of her very worst memory. She felt sick to the stomach even thinking about it. The closer they got, the worse she began to feel.

So much so that by the time they had left the plane and made their way to the low black Ferrari that had been parked ready for their arrival she was paler than pale, features drawn, eyes bruised by a deep sense of foreboding that was almost eating her up inside.

Sandro ignored it—of course he ignored it! she noted angrily as she sat beside him on the final leg of this journey down memory lane. He was the man on a mission, focused, blinkered. He didn't care what it was doing to her, only that he was determined to do it!

'I hate you,' she whispered at one point as they ground to a halt in Rome's famous traffic.

He ignored that too, preferring instead to switch on the in-car stereo. Orchestral music blared out from the radio: Verdi's 'Requiem'. It seemed so utterly fitting that she was surprised, therefore, when he quickly flicked it into CD mode so the much less provocative sound of a Mozart concerto filled the car.

He parked in a side-street beside his elegant apartment block, in one of those parking spaces that always seemed to magically open up for people like Sandro. Then he was shutting down the engine and climbing out of the car. By the time he had opened Joanna's door she was in a state of near collapse. His hand came out, dealing first with her seat belt for her, then firmly anchoring itself around her wrist to pull her out of the car.

She refused to look at him but she could feel his grimness, his dark sense of resolution, as he held onto her wrist while he shut the door and locked up the car.

Then——there it was: the aged ochre walls of a seventeenth-century building that had once been a beautiful *palazzo* and was now converted into three luxury apartments, one to each floor. Sandro had the top one; his bank owned the whole building, but of course its chairman lived at the top—which meant a lift was needed to get there.

His hand moved from her wrist to curve around her waist and, even as her spine tensed in tingling response, he set them moving, touching her, as he had promised, at every opportunity now, and she felt so brittle she wondered if her bones would actually snap if he squeezed her too tightly.

'Where's the luggage?' she asked tensely. Until that moment she had been too lost within her own growing nightmare to have noticed that they had traversed the whole airport and driven away in his car without collecting bags of any kind.

'There is none,' he answered coolly, still keeping her moving with that hand at her waist, so the full weight of his arm was angled across her rigid spine. 'We won't be needing it.'

They'd reached the apartment building entrance by now, stepping inside the luxurious foyer with its original wall frescos so beautifully renovated, like the priceless furniture surrounding them and the cleverly disguised lift hidden away behind its carved solid oak doors.

Joanna pushed a hand up to her trembling mouth as her stomach began to churn with an increasing frenzy. 'I feel sick,' she breathed.

Sandro ignored that too, grimly calling down the lift, then walking her inside it. It was palatial, red and golds mingling with oak, a gilded mirror fixed to its back wall.

She turned quickly away from her own haunted reflection, found her face pressed against Sandro's broad chest and left it there, trembling and shaking like a baby while he grimly started the lift, then closed both arms around her.

'I can't do this!' she choked into his chest, where she could feel the persistent throb of his beating heart.

'Shush,' he soothed, brushing his mouth across the top of her head. 'You can do it,' he insisted. 'And you will.'

The man with the mission had spoken, so no argument. She had never known him like this before, so rock-solidly determined that nothing seemed to get through to him.

The lift stopped. He helped her out, almost carried her across the deep red carpet to double doors set in two-foot-deep reveals that marked the true beginning of her nightmare.

One of Sandro's hands snaked out, briskly unlocking then pushing those big doors inwards. He stepped inside, attempting to take her with him, but she could not step over that wretched threshold as the bad memories began circling all around her.

This place, she was thinking tragically, this beautiful place so tastefully refurbished, in keeping with the building's great age and history. This large-roomed, high-ceilinged, exceptionally refined place where Sandro had brought her three years ago, with his ideals riding high on a buffeting cloud of anticipation—only to have them all brought crashing down at his disbelieving feet.

'I don't think I can bear it,' she whispered threadily.

She was clutching at him, one set of anguished fingers clawing at his shirt front while the other did the same to the back of his jacket.

'Shush, *cara*,' he soothed her yet again, his arm still curved around her, holding her securely anchored to his side. 'You must learn to trust me...'

Trust him? It wasn't a matter of trust! It was a matter of sheer self-preservation!

'Let me go to a hotel,' she pleaded. 'Just for tonight! Please, Sandro! I can't go in there!'

'You must know that the only way forward is to face the ghosts, Joanna,' he determined grimly. 'We will face them together. Now, come,' he urged, trying to draw her over that threshold while she dug her heels in like some recalcitrant donkey and refused point-blank to budge.

'Joanna, stop this,' he sighed in exasperation. 'You have no need to be afraid of this apartment!'

I do! she thought. I need to be quite this afraid of it.

'Let go of me or I shall s-start screaming,' she warned.

'But this is foolish!' he snapped, losing all patience with her. 'You are becoming hysterical!'

Hysterical? Yes, she was becoming hysterical. She didn't want to be here; she didn't want this—laying of ghosts he was threatening her with. She just wanted to—!

'I know, Joanna!' Sandro rasped out suddenly. 'You are hiding nothing by acting like this! For I know why you treated me the way you did the last time we were here together!'

He knew? For a short shocked moment she just stared at him blankly. Then—of course he didn't know! She completely denied the claim. He couldn't know. Nobody knew except for Molly—and she'd only ever known a tiny fraction of it!

Of course Sandro couldn't know—could he? 'I don't know what you're talking about,' she murmured shakily.

If anything, his face went all the harder, more determined, frighteningly determined. 'Yes, you do,' he insisted. 'I am talking about what happened to you the week before you married me. The night you were attacked.' He spelled it out brutally. 'On your way home from working late. I know, *cara*,' he repeated with a pained kind of gentle intensity. 'I know…'

It was like having a spring uncoil inside her and she jumped violently away from him. 'No,' she said, as her surroundings began to spin. 'You can't know.' She denied it absolutely. 'No.'

'Listen to me—' he urged.

'No!' she began to back away from him, face white, eyes gone slightly wild, while Sandro watched her with a kind of distressed understanding that almost sliced her in two. 'No,' she said again when he took a step towards her. 'You don't know,' she insisted. 'I don't want you to know!'

'But, Joanna—'

'Not you, Sandro. Not you!' she cried out in such heart-rending agony that he seemed to catch it in his chest like a blow.

Her stumbling backward steps took her all the way to the wall opposite the doors to his apartment, but still she kept going, sideways now, tracking herself along the wall while Sandro stood there watching her with such grim compassion in his eyes that she wanted to die, wanted to shrivel up where she was; she wanted the floor to open up and swallow her whole.

'Don't look at me like that,' she breathed, feeling trapped and helpless and so exposed she could have been standing here naked, while her fevered mind filled with looming dark shadows, lurid bulks of silently moving flesh leering at her, laughing, sniggering.

And then there was Sandro, coming towards her, slowly, stealthily, like a man approaching a frightened animal. 'It had to come out into the open!' he uttered in a harsh, driven voice that pleaded even as it whipped her. 'You cannot—*I cannot* keep it hidden any longer! *Madre di dio!*' he sighed. 'Can you not see what it is doing to you?'

'No.' Refusing to listen, refusing to accept, she shook her head. 'You don't know,' she repeated. 'I don't want you to know.'

'But why?' he demanded in pained bemusement. 'Why can you not trust me with this? Why do you need to shut me out!'

Why was easy, but she was in no state to answer him. Her tracking fingertips made contact with wooden framework, sending her face twisting sideways to where she found herself staring through the open doors to the waiting lift. Somewhere inside her head there was a strange buzzing sound, and in the distance Sandro's voice, low and deep and oddly constricted, was saying something about them going into the apartment and talking about it.

But she didn't want to talk about *it*! She didn't want to be here in this place!

Escape.

She had to escape before it all came crashing down on her.

'Joanna—'

She made a dive for those open lift doors, almost hurling herself inside them.

And suddenly there it was, the big black hole she had spent so many months carefully skirting around. Only this time it claimed her. She tumbled headlong into it, falling—falling for what seemed like for ever, until eventually there was nothing, nothing but a strange feeling of utter weightlessness and the blackness, that terrible, all-enveloping, mind-numbing blackness...

The climb back to reality was a long and arduous one. Every time she thought she might be getting there, the rim of the dark hole would crumble beneath her grasping fingers and she would slide back down again, sobbing in anguish and in fear, her teeth gritting in frustration. Her fingers scrambled to catch hold of something, anything, to stop her falling, so she could begin the laborious climb out once again.

Sometimes she feared she would never make it, that she was destined to spend the rest of her life climbing the steep walls of this hole, only to slide down again. And sometimes ghastly familiar faces would come leering at her over the rim, laughing and taunting her wasted efforts. Sometimes it was the leering young face of a skinhead yobbo; sometimes it was Arthur Bates, his greedy eyes warning her what to expect if she did ever get out of her dark prison.

Then Molly would come, pushing those awful men out of the way and smiling reassuringly at her, urging her upwards with a hand stretched out for her to try and catch hold of. But the hand always stayed those few precious few inches out of reach. 'It isn't fair,' she whimpered fretfully. 'It just isn't fair. I can't reach you.'

'Shush,' a soothing voice murmured. 'I am here. I have hold of you.'

And she frowned, because that voice wasn't Molly's voice; it was Sandro's. She looked up, saw him leaning over the rim of the hole and reaching down for her. His arm was longer than Molly's, he managed to grab a hold on her wrist, pull her up. Up and up. He bodily yanked her over the rim of the hole, then tossed her to ground which was too far away for her to tumble back in.

It was such a relief, such a wonderful relief, that she

smiled and thanked him. He covered her up with a blanket. 'Go to sleep,' he commanded. 'You are safe here.'

And she really did feel safe at last, so safe that she drifted into a blissfully peaceful and uncluttered sleep where she felt warm and protected by the arms enfolding her.

Joanna opened her eyes to find sunlight seeping in through a silk draped floor-to-ceiling window onto a cream and pale blue colour-washed room. It was a lovely room, she decided sleepily. She liked the high ceiling and the feeling of space it seemed to offer. She liked the subtle use of the two pastel colours; they were cool and restful. She wondered who the room belonged to.

Where was she? She frowned, having a hazy recollection of something terrible happening, but as for what, she couldn't quite manage to recall at the moment.

Then a grimly protracted voice murmured flatly, 'How do you feel?' making her head turn sharply on the pillow to find Sandro reclining in an easy chair beside the bed.

His dark head was turned her way, his brown eyes fixed on her with absolutely no expression whatsoever. Gone was the electrifying power-dressing suit she had last seen him wearing, and in its place were casual linen trousers and a plain black polo shirt.

Power-dressing, she repeated to herself, and suddenly it all came back in a horrified rush. The memories, where she was, why she was lying here like this, and why Sandro was sitting there like that, looking as though he had been there for hours—hours just watching her—knowing...

'What happened?' she asked, desperately playing for time while she tried to come to terms with what had taken place earlier.

'You don't remember?'

She remembered almost everything in razor-sharp detail, but to admit to that meant facing it, and at the moment she couldn't bear to face it. 'Not much,' she lied. 'Only a vague recollection of you and I arguing. Did we have a row?'

'You could say that.' He smiled an odd twist of a smile. 'Then you—became ill.'

Became ill, she mused balefully. She had not merely become ill, she had jumped into the screaming pits of Hell rather than face up to what Sandro had claimed he knew about her.

'Where am I?'

'In Rome. In my apartment,' he said, eyeing her narrowly. 'Where you collapsed. When you showed no sign of recovering, I called in a doctor.'

A doctor? Oh, good grief! How long had she been lying here like this? 'And he said—what?' she enquired, very warily.

His eyes made a critical sweep of her too-slender shape beneath the thin layer of bedding, and for the first time she realised that she was wearing nothing more than what felt like a tee shirt.

Her eyelashes lowered, quickly covering a burst of flurried heat because she was suddenly acutely aware that someone had undressed her and put her to bed like this—and that person could only have been Sandro.

'He called it a combination of too much stress,' he answered, 'and not eating enough food to keep a mouse alive.'

Sandro—had Sandro undressed her?

'I've had the 'flu recently,' she said, pushing a decidedly shaky hand to her brow so she could hide behind it. 'Maybe it was that.'

He didn't answer, made absolutely no comment, and she didn't dare look at him to see if she could discover what he was thinking.

'I'm thirsty,' she announced, trying to moisten paper-dry lips with an equally dry tongue.

He was instantly on his feet and stepping over to a

bedside table where a crystal jug full of iced water and a glass tumbler stood glinting in the rich sunlight. While he poured the water she pulled herself into a sitting position, only to stop, pushing her hand back to her brow, when her head began swimming dizzily.

Sandro stopped what he was doing to reach out a hand towards her. She saw it coming and instinctively stiffened in readiness for its electrifying touch. It hovered there in mid-air for a long second while her teeth gritted and the silence in the room became thick with tension.

Then the hand diverted, going to pick up the pillows from behind her and resettling them so she could lean back against them. She did so out of sheer necessity, face pale, eyes closed, feeling so weak inside it was almost pathetic.

Silently Sandro waited. When she could stand it no longer she opened her eyes, and honed them onto the glass full of iced water he was holding; she simply stared at it, wondering how she was going to take it from him without letting her fingers brush against his.

'I am not a monster,' he said grimly, knowing exactly what she was thinking.

'Thank you,' she mumbled, feeling cruel and heartless, and forced herself to take the glass.

She wanted to apologise, but when she did that it tended to make him angry, so instead she said nothing and sipped at the refreshing water, wishing he would sit down again, because when he stood over her like this she felt so intimidated. Wishing he would go away because she needed some time to herself to come to terms with yesterday's catastrophic developments.

Then a frown touched her brow. *Was* it only yesterday she had walked herself right into Sandro's power again? She had no real idea what day it was, or of the time, except the sunlight was suggesting to her that this was at least one new day. Maybe there had been others.

Maybe she had been lying here for days and days, fighting to climb out of that awful dark pit.

Then, no, she told herself, as the nerve-ends throughout her whole system began to tighten. She must not let herself think about those dreadful dreams or she might start to fall apart all over again.

'How long have I been here?' she asked Sandro

He sat down again, which was marginally better than having him stand over her. Then he really brought the whole lot bursting back out in the open by informing her with super-silk sardonism, 'Today is the second day of your new life, *cara*. You spent what was left of your first day half-comatose, you see...'

See? Oh, she saw everything! And nearly dropped the glass. She hadn't fooled him in the slightest. He knew she remembered and he wasn't going to let her get away with lying about it!

'I think I hate you,' she whispered miserably.

'*Si,*' he sighed. 'So you are continually telling me.'

Then suddenly he was back on his feet again, taking the glass of water from her and setting it aside so he could come and lean over her, much in the same way he had done yesterday, when he'd meant to make a very important point.

'But don't think——' he warned, dipping his head to catch her eyes and, when she quickly lowered them, placing a hand on her chin to *make* her look at him—make her look and see the grim determination written in his own glinting dark eyes. 'Don't think that your lousy opinion of me or my own lousy guilty conscience for putting you into this damn bed the way I did is going to reverse what actually happened yesterday, because it is not! Now I have you out in the open, you are staying out,' he vowed.

Then he straightened, turned and walked out of the room, leaving her sitting there wondering balefully what he had in store for her if he could still be this angry so many hours later.

'Oh, damn it,' she sighed as her head began to swim again.

What in heaven's name had she let herself in for by setting herself up for this? She didn't need it—didn't want it! And she was as sure as anything that Sandro couldn't want to put them both through this kind of hell a second time!

It had been bad enough the first time around, she recalled heavily. Her loving him, needing him, wanting him so badly but unable to let him touch her. His hurt, his frustration, his soul-crushing bewilderment at why she was reacting to him like that!

Why should he understand it? The week before they were due to be married she had barely been able to keep her hands off him. Then he'd flown here, to Rome, to put in place the finishing touches on the wholesale transfer of his head offices to London—because Joanna needed to stay in London until Molly was old enough, and financially independent enough, to survive there on her own.

Molly...

The pretty, pale blue-washed ceiling clouded out of focus. In Joanna's view, Molly had been the absolute opposite of her more determined and fiercely independent big sister. But then, Joanna had needed to be, because, at the tender age of eighteen, she had taken over full responsibility for her fourteen-year-old sister, when their mother had died after a long, long illness which had left them with no one else to turn to; four years before that Grandpa had gone, taking with him the only period in her life when Joanna could have said with any certainty that she had felt truly cared for, instead of being the one who did the caring.

But that was another story, one not worth rehashing,

because she still missed Grandpa and his tiny small-holding in Kent as much as she still missed Molly.

They had been half-sisters really, born by different fathers to a mother who, by her own admission, had loved many men—though none of them well enough to want to tie herself down. And, in the circular way life tends to turn, both Joanna and Molly had secretly yearned for the so-called old-fashioned and conventional close family unit, with a father as well as a mother to claim as their own.

It was not to be. A small sigh shook her. Consequently, growing up had been tougher for Molly and herself than most—though not so tough as some. They'd had a home of sorts: a rented flat in the East End district of London where their mother had taken them to live after Grandpa died. Their mother had worked all hours to keep them reasonably fed, clothed and healthy, and Joanna had taken care of Molly—then of her mother and Molly, when their mother eventually became ill.

So, continuing to take care of Molly after their mother had gone had not been any real hardship. She'd been used to doing it. They'd stayed on in the flat their mother had rented, and Joanna had started working all the hours she could to keep that same roof over their heads while Molly finished her education.

Molly had been clever. She'd been quiet, shy and studious, and incredibly pretty: blonde-haired and blue eyed with sweet gentle features. Joanna had harboured a secret dream where Molly would go on to university, make something of herself, then meet a wonderful man who would treasure her baby sister for the rest of her life.

Only, it was Joanna who had met the wonderful man. It was as if Sandro had stepped right out of her dreams for Molly and had become her own dream.

It had been magical. Once again, she was transported back to that tiny back-street Italian restaurant where she'd worked at in the evenings. He'd been superbly dressed, beautifully groomed and so handsome he took her breath away. She had never in her life come face to face with a man like Alessandro.

He'd come to visit Vito and had ended up staying all evening to flirt with Joanna instead, seemingly fascinated by the pretty red-haired waitress who was so bright and cheerful, and contrarily shy when he tried turning on his charismatic Italian charm.

He'd waited for her until she'd finished work that night and walked her home. Within a month he was like a permanent fixture—at the restaurant, and at the small flat she'd shared with Molly. And Joanna had been so blindly in love with him, she hadn't really thought much about who he was or what he was. It hadn't seemed to matter that he drove a fast car and wore designer clothes. Or that he was always having to fly off somewhere on business. He wasn't standoffish, though he had been critical of the fact that she'd held down two jobs—working during the day-time in a wine bar and nights at the restaurant—but only because it hadn't left her much time to be with him.

The problems had started when he'd asked her to marry him and come to live with him, here in Rome. She couldn't leave Molly, who had only been seventeen then, and had had another full year in education before Joanna could even begin thinking of her own future.

He'd accepted it—amazing, now, as she looked back and thought about how Sandro had accepted every obstacle she'd tossed in his way: 'Molly needs me here; I won't desert her after all we've been through together.'

'Fine,' he'd said. 'Then I will have to find another way.' And he had. He'd decided to move himself to London. 'I will move heaven and earth if that is what it will take for you and I to be together,' he'd explained.

Then there was the night when she'd shyly told him that she was still a virgin. Later she'd wished she'd kept her silly mouth shut, because he had been about to make love to her then, finally and fully. For the first time in weeks they had actually managed to grab a full evening at her flat without Molly, because she was staying at a friend's house. So there they'd been, half undressed and wonderfully lost in each other, when it had suddenly occurred to her that she should warn him.

He'd been so stunned, then so damned pleased about it that she'd been almost offended. 'I can't believe it.' He'd grinned at her. 'I have a real live angel in my arms and she's going to be all mine!'

'I'm no angel!' she'd protested. 'Just a very busy girl who's not had time to get into heavy relationships!'

She should have seen the writing on the wall then, when he'd suddenly changed towards her, stopped being so passionate, stopped trying to seduce her at every opportunity he could get, and begun treating her like some rare object he had to cosset and protect from the big bad wolf lurking inside him.

'You are special,' he'd explained. 'I want our wedding night to be special. I want you to wear white when you marry me and I want to stand beside you and think, This woman is special and she is coming to me pure of body! What more could any man wish for in the woman he loves?'

And that was when she'd begun to worry that Sandro loved her virginity more than he loved her!

But she had been busy, still working two jobs because she was stubbornly insisting on paying for her own bridal gown and trousseau, and time had been racing by, so she hadn't particularly dwelt on his obsession with her virginal state because she'd had more important things to think about—like being nervous about meeting his very large family, or moving into his lovely home in Belgravia, where she'd felt like a duck in a swan's nest from the moment she'd first stepped over the threshold. Then there'd been Molly to worry about, because she was suddenly making noises about not going on to university, about getting a job instead and maybe even a flat to share with some friends. And Joanna had been worried that Molly was saying all of this because she felt she should be leaving Joanna and Sandro alone to start their marriage.

So she'd been pretty lost in worries that night she travelled on the Underground home from work a week before her wedding day. Too preoccupied to be alerted to what was brewing around her on that train.

Afterwards—well, afterwards she'd found her whole world had come tumbling down, bringing Sandro's world tumbling down with it.

Could he really be serious about thrusting them both back into that kind of living breathing hell again? she wondered heavily. Did he think anything would be different this time just because he believed he now knew why she had been like that with him?

Well, he was wrong, because no one knew the real truth about what had happened that night because she had never told the truth, not even to Molly. And nothing was going to change. It couldn't—she couldn't.

The bedroom door swung inwards, allowing Sandro to walk in carrying a tray loaded with coffee and a rack of freshly made toast.

He looked different again, dressed for business in an iron-grey suit and white shirt, a dark silk tie knotted at his throat.

'I have to go out for a short while,' he said as he placed the tray across her lap. 'If you want me for anything, then the number of my mobile phone is written on a pad by the telephone.'

'The prisoner is allowed to make telephone calls, then?' she said caustically.

He didn't answer, his mouth straightening. 'I will be about an hour,' he informed her instead. 'Try to eat, then rest. We will talk again later.'

Talk! Talk about what? she wondered apprehensively

as she watched him depart again. The past? The present? The future?

Well, she didn't want to talk about any of them. She didn't want to eat. She didn't want to rest. She just wanted to get out of here!

Without warning, the old panic hit.

She needed to get out of this apartment, where bad memories lurked in every corner! She needed time to herself, to think, go over what had already happened and how she was going to deal with what was promising to come next. But, above all, she needed to do it now while Sandro wasn't standing guard over her!

CHAPTER SIX

PUSHING the breakfast tray from her lap, Joanna scrambled quickly out of the bed, only to land swaying on her feet, feeling about as weak as a newborn kitten.

A quick shower might help, she decided, glancing around the room until she spied a door that promised to be an adjoining bathroom.

Ten minutes later she was back in the bedroom, feeling better—clean, refreshed, more alert—wrapped in a snowy white bathrobe she'd found hanging conveniently on the bathroom door. It smelled faintly of Sandro, that subtle tangy scent that was so uniquely him. But then, she grimaced to herself, her whole body now smelled like Sandro since she had just used his soap.

Which led her to another troubling concept—Sandro's soap, Sandro's bathroom, Sandro's bed!

The bed she had just been lying in had to be Sandro's bed! But, if that was the case, then it was not the same bedroom he had taken her to the last time he had brought her here. That room had been bigger than this one, more opulent, and fifty times more frightening.

She shuddered, remembering why the room had been so frightening; then grimly shoved the memory aside while she dealt with her next most pressing problem— namely, some clothes to wear.

No luggage, she remembered. No need for it, Sandro had said. Did that mean he really did intend to keep her here as a prisoner until he had managed to make this a real marriage?

Alarm shot through her, lending her limbs the required impetus to open wardrobe and cupboard doors; she was expecting to find Sandro's clothes and frowned when she didn't.

Instead they were full of the most stylish women's clothes she had ever laid eyes on—even during her one-year long marriage to Sandro she had never owned outfits as stylish as these!

But then, she had always insisted on choosing her clothes herself, stubbornly refusing to let him spend gross amounts on her because she hadn't felt that she deserved it. So, although she had been forced to accept the odd designer outfit Sandro bought for her himself—like the Dior suit she had worn yesterday—most of her clothes had been good but not designer-label, and nothing—nothing like the garments hanging here.

Who did they belong too? she asked herself frowningly, then felt her spine stiffen as the answer came to her.

Did these beautiful clothes belong to his very discreet mistress?

She felt sick again suddenly, too sick to think beyond the need to get away from here. So, with heart pounding and hands trembling, she dragged a pair of denims and a tiny white tee shirt off their hangers, and almost sank to the ground in relief when she noticed they still possessed their shop tags—which meant that all these clothes were brand-new.

They also fitted her slender figure as if they had been bought for her, which led to the next uncomfortable suspicion—that, if they did not belong to his mistress, he must have had them brought here specifically for her.

New clothes, new life.

The two fitted together so neatly that the old sense of wild panic hit all over again, and she scrambled urgently around, looking for something to wear on her feet. She found a pair of lightweight leather slip-ons and hurriedly pushed her bare feet into them. Her freshly-shampooed hair slid like a curtain around her face, drying quickly of its own accord in the heat Rome was basking in—while London still shivered.

At last she was ready to walk out of the room and down the hall to the apartment's main doors. It took mere seconds to make it as far as the lift, only then to use up precious minutes having to talk herself into using the damned thing.

It's either that or stay here, she told herself grimly. Because she couldn't see any sign of a stairwell in the vicinity.

Frustration bit hard into her lily-white cowardice, sharp white teeth doing the same to her full bottom lip. Oh, stop being so pathetic! she told herself angrily. One bad experience in a lift didn't make all lifts evil places!

Still, even as she stepped forward and made herself press the call button, she was half hoping that the lift wouldn't come. But there was a whirring sound and a click as it arrived at its destination. The doors slid open and Joanna looked warily inside, memories of what had happened the last time these doors had stood open in front of her like this mingling with all her other wretched lift memories.

With a deep breath, she made herself walk forward, turn to face the console, then sent up a tense finger to stab at the 'down' button. The doors swished shut. She closed her eyes, felt the lift start to move and curled her hands into tight fists at her sides as her heart began to hammer.

Oh, why did it have to be like this? she asked herself tragically. Why did she have to live in fear of lifts, or have to run away from a man who had never once lifted a single finger towards her in anger?

A man she loved, a man she cared for; a man who had once loved her enough to move heaven and earth just so that he could be with her! It wasn't fair—it just wasn't fair!

The lift stopped. Her eyes flicked open, bright blue

and wretched, because she'd suddenly realised that she couldn't do it; she just couldn't run out on him like this!

The doors parted; one of her hands snaked up to press the 'up' button...

'Well, well,' a smoothly sardonic voice drawled. 'Now, why isn't this as big a surprise as it should be?'

He was leaning against the lift's outer casing, smiling at her but in an angry way—very angry; she could see the twin fires burning in his dark eyes.

'How...?'

'How did I know you were on your way down here?' he accurately interpreted. 'Because each time this lift is used an alarm sounds in the concierge's office—where I was sitting enjoying a cup of coffee and a pleasant chat,' he explained with acid bite.

'I...'

'You were on your way to look for me?' he suggested lazily. 'How nice.'

'No,' she denied, flushing slightly. 'I...'

'Because you missed me so much, you could not bear to be away from me for a single moment longer.' He nodded sagely. 'I am most flattered.'

'Will you stop finishing my sentences for me?' she snapped. 'That was not what I was going to say!'

'I also see you are feeling much better,' he drawled. 'For the shrew is back.'

'I wasn't leaving,' she retorted, wondering why she had changed her mind about running when, really, two seconds in his company was enough to make any woman run!

'Just working off your phobia about lifts.' He nodded again, clearly not believing her. 'How brave, *cara*.'

Joanna sighed and leaned a defeated shoulder against the lift wall. 'I only wanted some fresh air, Sandro,' she told him heavily.

'Fresh air? Of course. Why did I not think of that?'

And before she could react, his hand snaked out to catch her wrist and with a tug he had her out of the lift.

'W-where are we going?' she demanded as he began pulling her towards the rear of the apartment block.

'For fresh air,' he answered laconically. 'As the lady requested.'

Then he was pushing open a door that took them outside into the sensually warm dappled sunlight, and a cobbled courtyard, high-walled on three sides with the building itself forming the fourth. In its centre the requisite Italian fountain was sprinkling fine droplets of water into a rippling pond. The walls hung with colour, all brilliant shades, and the sunlight filtered down through the spread branches of a fig tree onto a stone bench seat and table set beneath it.

'Is this fresh enough for you?' Sandro enquired lightly as he pulled her over to the bench and virtually forced her to sit down on it before leaning his hips against the table behind him. He folded his arms, then proceeded to view her with enough mockery in his eyes to make her wince and blush furiously.

'I was not running away from you!' she tried a second time. 'I—I was going to,' she then reluctantly admitted, 'but then I changed my mind.'

'Why?'

Why? Oh, hell. 'I haven't got anywhere to go, have I?' she shrugged.

'And you only remembered that on the way down here?'

'Yes,' she sighed.

He nodded his dark head as though she had just confirmed every bad opinion he harboured about her. Then, in one of those complete turnabouts in manner which he could make to such devastating effect, he smiled—just smiled—and her heart turned over. The man was too charismatic for his own good!

'You're precious,' he murmured as he dipped a hand

into his jacket pocket and came out with something. 'I adore you for it. Tell me what you think of that,' he invited amiably, offering her what looked like a glossy magazine.

Bemused, confused, most definitely wary, because his tone had gone from bitingly sarcastic to tender so quickly that she just didn't trust it, she took the magazine while her eyes remained fixed on his handsome face.

His expression told her nothing.

But then again, she mused as she lowered her eyes to study what was now in her hands, that face of his was just too riveting for anyone to see past its beauty and read what was going on in his mind!

She was staring at a glossy coloured brochure, not a magazine, she realised. A brochure with a photograph of a lovely red-roofed villa set in the middle of the most delightful surroundings.

For some reason it reminded her of Grandpa. She wasn't sure why, unless it was because she had been thinking about him earlier; she could draw no comparison between Grandpa's very modest smallholding and the aerial view of very large country estate she was seeing in this picture.

The villa itself was a low, rambling place, with yellowing walls and green paint-washed wooden frames to the windows and doors. There were outbuildings, a swimming pool and several large fenced paddocks, not to mention fruit groves and long rows of grape vines spreading out over rolling countryside.

A magical place, she decided, set in magical surroundings.

Puzzled as to why Sandro wanted her to look at this, she opened the brochure's cover, expecting to gain enlightenment from its inner pages. But the print was in Italian—though there were more photographs, of the inside of what looked like a commercial wine cellar lined with huge old-fashioned oak barrels, and another one showing a beautifully cared for stable block.

'Are you thinking of investing in a vineyard?' she asked in a guess, since the brochure reminded her of those you found in the very best estate agents.

'Wine-making is not one of my family's interests,' Sandro answered reflectively. 'As you know, we are bankers by tradition. But I stayed close to this place a while back and was enchanted by it. What do you think?'

'I think it's beautiful,' she answered softly. 'All that blue sky and open space and peace and tranquillity...'

'No buses, no trains,' he wryly tagged on. 'No shops within miles of the place...'

'No people?' she asked.

'Local people, who have worked the land for as far back as their family history will take them. But, no,' he said quietly. 'No people in the way that you mean.'

'Perfect, in fact, then,' she murmured wistfully.

'You could say that,' he agreed.

The mobile phone in his pocket began to ring then, and as he turned his attention to answering whoever was calling him Joanna got to her feet and moved a couple of steps away to look over the brochure in relative privacy. As a barrage of friendly Italian began to wash over her, she heard the name of the person Sandro was speaking to.

'Ah, Guido!' he greeted. *'Ciao! Ciao...!'*

After that she was lost, but the name Guido was familiar to her—very familiar. He was just one of Sandro's many relatives—a cousin who worked as a lawyer for the Bonetti Bank. He was also the man who had stood witness for Sandro at their wedding.

Guido wasn't built in the same physical mould as Sandro, nor did he wield the same power. But he was a nice enough man. He had been keen to like her because she was marrying Sandro, all of whose family had been eager to like the woman their great chief had chosen to spend the rest of his life with.

Even Sandro's mother, she recalled, her eyes glazing over as her mind built a picture of Sandro's slender, dark-haired mother, who had been so warm in welcoming Joanna into her family. Her husband was dead, so she'd poured all of her love into her only child. Anything Sandro wanted, his mother wanted for him too. 'You are my daughter now,' she had said kindly. 'Make my son happy and I will be forever your friend.'

But Joanna had not made her son happy.

'*Si—Si,*' Sandro murmured, bringing her attention swinging back to him in time to watch him grin before he continued in another fast spate of Italian.

She hadn't seen him this at ease with himself since she'd come back into his life, she noted bleakly. Hadn't seen that attractive grin warm his mouth, or heard that happy lilt in the deep bass of his sensual voice.

Seeing that grin come alive now made her wish she knew what he was talking about; she wished she'd taken the time to learn his language so maybe *she* could make him smile like that occasionally.

But she didn't need a grasp of Italian to make Sandro smile, she recalled. It took her simple desire to please; that was all. Something she'd once used to have, but now was no longer allowed to have.

This beautiful country estate pleased him, she reflected as she looked back at the brochure. She had seen the pleasure in his face as he'd looked at it, seen the desire to own a place like this.

'So, shall I purchase it or not?'

She blinked, not realising he had finished his conversation and was concentrating on her again.

'You're the investment expert,' she said, passing the brochure back to him with a dismissiveness that brought the old frown back to his face.

'You don't like it?'

'I think its beautiful; I told you that,' she snapped, half hating herself for raining on his parade like this.

'Good.' Casually he put the brochure aside. 'Because I have just closed a deal on it, via Guido,' he announced, beginning to smile again. 'So, if you are feeling up to it, *cara*, we will drive up there tomorrow and look over our new home.'

Predictably, Joanna froze while Sandro remained leaning where he was, ruefully watching it happen.

'I don't understand,' she whispered finally.

'Yes, you do,' he parried in a soft-toned taunt that sent warning quivers shooting down her spine. 'For tomorrow will be the third day of your new life,' he chanted, in what was becoming his most effective barb to keep her mind fully concentrated on who was in control around here. 'It will begin with a drive out of Rome towards the *Orvieto* region, and end on the estate, with just you, me, and our marriage to work on.'

'No.' The protest was purely instinctive, as was the way she was already stiffening up, making to move right away from him—

But Sandro stopped her with a hand on her arm.

'No more running from what you don't want to face, Joanna,' he warned. 'That tightly closed door in your head is now open and I mean to keep it that way.'

'And I have no say in the matter, I suppose,' she bit back, trying to sound shrewish and only managing to sound anxious.

'Not while you still fight me, no,' he confirmed. 'You see, I know the problem now, so I intend to deal with it.'

The problem, she repeated to herself. The problem which was Joanna's aversion to sex! But he didn't know the real problem—didn't know even half of it!

'I need to go and—' Once again she tried to move away.

'No.' Once more Sandro stopped her, the hand on her

arm firmly drawing her in front of him and keeping her there with both hands spanning her narrow waist while he studied the strain written in her face through very grim eyes.

Not angry, but grim. There was a definite distinction, because his anger gave her something to spark on, but his grimness only made her want to break down and cry.

'I won't let you touch me!' she flashed, eyes snapping everywhere they could go, so long as they did not settle on him.

He didn't answer, he just kept her standing there in front of him in the dappling sunshine while he moved his eyes over her, from her freshly washed hair to the clothes she had pulled on in her haste to get away from him.

Now she almost wished she'd run naked through the streets of Rome rather than having wasted those extra minutes agonising over whose clothes she was going to have to wear.

'You know,' he remarked suddenly, 'you have the best pair of legs I have ever set eyes on. Those jeans do the most exciting things to my libido...'

So low-voiced and sensual, so evocative of a time when he'd used to say things like that to her all the time. She hadn't realised how precious those kind of words were to her until she no longer dared to listen to them.

'Please, don't,' she choked, feeling desperate, feeling flustered, feeling other senses begin to disturb her oh, so fragile equilibrium with low, droning vibrations of awareness to him.

But he only gave a small shake of his head and drew her even closer, parting his legs and wedging her between two long, strong muscular thighs. Her breath caught; her breast-tips were ready and waiting to sting into life at this mere hint that their most favourite stimulus was so close again.

His expression was so intense, so—Italian, a raw animal sexuality seeming to ooze from every silk-smooth golden pore. 'You smell of me,' he detected softly. 'I find it most alluring...'

Oh, please, she prayed. Don't let him do this to me! 'This is crazy,' she jerked out in rising panic. 'I don't know why you think it will be any different now than it was before!'

'Tell me then, why you gambled away all of that money?' he countered.

The money? What did the money have to do with this?

'I told you why,' she murmured distractedly, trying to prise away his imprisoning hands with her own. She couldn't budge him, not one bit. 'Sandro—please!' she cried out in stark desperation.

He ignored it. 'Your Mr Bates was of the opinion that you went about losing that money with a vengeance,' he informed her. 'With your eyes wide open to the eventual consequences.'

'And you believed him?' she charged, feeling sick to her stomach at the very sound of Bates' name. 'You of all people should know that had to be a damned lie!'

'You would assume so,' he agreed. 'But then—I have never met a man more likely to send any woman screaming for the nearest place of safety...'

She realised then just what he was implying, and her eyes began to flash with stunned incredulity. 'You think I got myself into that mess deliberately so I had an excuse to come begging from you?' She gasped at his absolute arrogance.

'Did you?' he challenged outright. 'Or was it more complex than that?' he then suggested, eyes narrowed, like two hot lasers trying to probe into the very darkest part of her brain. 'Did Arthur Bates or do I bear a close resemblance to the man who attacked you, *cara*?'

Joanna went white, her whole stance stone-still for the

few stunning seconds it took her to thoroughly absorb what he was actually suggesting here.

Then the words came, hot and hard and crucifyingly pungent, bursting forth from the very depths of her vilified psyche. 'Two,' she corrected. 'It was *two* men who *raped* me, *caro*!' she sliced at him with a stinging black mockery. 'In a *lift*, if you want the full truth about it!'

And while he leaned there, seemingly locked into total immobility by what she had just thrown at him, Joanna knocked his imprisoning arms aside, pushed herself right away from him and made for the door back into the building, with nausea rising in her throat, the dire need to get away from everything giving her shaken limbs the impetus to carry her quickly.

She actually made it as far as the front entrance before Sandro's hand snaked out to grab her arm and pull her to a jarring stop.

'Don't touch me!' she bit out, angrily knocking the hand away again.

Sandro said nothing, his face white and drawn. But he took hold of her arm again and led her back to the lift. The doors stood open; he drew her inside. Joanna whirled away from him to stand glaring at the panelled wall while he grimly hit the 'up' button.

The doors closed. A thick silence throbbed in the very fabric of the walls surrounding them. Joanna closed her eyes and held her breath, and this time it had nothing to do with her aversion to travelling in lifts!

They stopped and she swung around, hair flying, eyes burning with a rage beyond anything she'd ever experienced before. She completely ignored Sandro's existence as she stalked out of the lift and back into the apartment.

'Forgive me,' he murmured huskily from somewhere behind her.

'May you burn in hell,' she replied, and found herself walking as if by instinct into what her subconscious mind must have remembered was the drawing room of this super-elegant place. With the same unerring accuracy she found the drinks cabinet, snapped it open, poured herself a neat gin, then swallowed it.

'I only knew you had been attacked on your way home from work,' Sandro persisted. 'I knew none of the details. Molly refused to discuss them with me. I jumped in with both feet, and I apologise. It was both cruel and thoughtless.'

Molly, she repeated angrily to herself. It had to be Molly who had broken a confidence and told him, because no one else had ever known! And even Molly had never known any of what she had just spat at Sandro.

'She was worried about you, Joanna,' he explained, seeming to need to defend her own sister. 'She was worried that if you did not talk about it to someone you were going to make yourself ill.'

'So, because I wouldn't discuss it with her, she decided to discuss it with you.' Joanna pushed the gin to her lips, but her hand was shaking so badly that the glass chattered against her teeth so she pulled it away again.

'What did you expect her to do?' Sandro sighed, her attitude sparking his anger. 'You shut her out! You shut me out! The two people who loved you!'

'I shut myself *in*!' she responded angrily, swinging around to glare at him through eyes so hard and bright they actually looked dangerous. 'It was *my* problem— *my* choice how I dealt with it!'

'It was *our* problem!' he retaliated harshly. 'I had a right to know why the woman I'd believed loved me suddenly developed that sickening aversion to me!'

'And what was I supposed to say to you, Sandro?' she challenged him. 'Oh, by the way, I was raped on my way home from work last week, so don't worry if I can't let you touch me. It isn't personal! Would that have done?'

'You should have trusted me enough to expect love

and support from me! I could at least have given you that!'

'Are you joking?' she gasped, slamming the gin glass down with enough force to shatter it with the power of her anger. 'Sandro—you had me up on some kind of damn pedestal! You went on and on about how wonderful it was that I was still a virgin! How you wanted our wedding night to be perfect—pristine white—no shadows!'

Her voice cracked. He spun his back to her, his shoulders bunched, his body stiff. It made it easier; she could shout out all the ugliness to his back much better than she could do to his face.

'I was raped one week before our perfect wedding!' she cried. 'You were here in Rome! I was deep in shock! It was h-horrible!' She shuddered, her arms wrapping tightly around herself. 'I didn't want to remember it, never mind talk about it! I wanted to pretend it hadn't happened and keep floating through the perfect dream marriage you had mapped out for us!'

'So you thought you could marry me, come to my bed and pretend you were exactly what I was expecting?' He spun back to lance her with embittered eyes and she lowered her gaze.

'Yes,' she sighed. 'Something like that.'

'But when it came to it you could not even let me touch you, never mind make love to you. So the perfection was ruined anyway. You should have told me then,' he directed. 'Explained then. Absolved me of blame for your revulsion! But instead you let me suffer,' he rasped out thickly, 'not knowing what it was about me you could not tolerate! What you did, Joanna, was punish me for the sins of those animals who attacked you!'

He was oh, so deplorably right! So much so that she suddenly decided she couldn't take any more! 'I don't want to talk about it,' she said, spinning jerkily towards the door.

'No!' The refusal seemed to explode violently from somewhere deep down inside his angry breast, pulling her to a tense standstill. 'We will deal with this now!' he insisted. 'We will drag it all out into the open and kick each other to death with it, if we have to! But we will deal with this now, Joanna. Right here and now!'

'What more do you want from me?' she reeled back to blast at him. 'Absolution of all blame? Well, you have it!' she declared, with a wild wave of one badly shaking hand, eyes glinting, hair shimmering, slender body quivering with a furious provocation. 'I was at fault! I didn't trust you enough to confide in you! I punished you for other men's sins! I made your life a misery!'

'You broke my heart and did not even notice,' he tagged on gruffly.

That rocked Joanna on the very axis upon which she stood. She couldn't believe he had actually said it! It was such an awful, awful thing for a man like him to openly admit!

Yet there was no longer any anger in his lean, dark expression, no biting regret that he had been driven to voice such a dreadful admission. He was simply responding to his own dictum and telling it as it was.

The truth, the full truth and whole truth—even if it was a gut-wrenching truth!

'But you did more than that,' he went on in a voice suddenly devoid of all emotion. 'You despoiled me, *cara*. As surely as those men despoiled you without a qualm, you emasculated me with your revulsion. You stripped me naked of my pride in myself as a man—in my manhood! You scorned me as a lover and you revolted at my touch. You recognise these effects? They ring bells for you?'

'Oh, my God,' she whispered in shaken comprehension.

'Now we will discuss cause and effect for you, if you please.' As always, when his emotions were under pressure, his near perfect English slipped into a bone-melting Italian inflection. 'For I think I have earned the right to know exactly what happened to make you treat me like that!'

MICHELLE REID   115

Sara, but near perfect English slipped into a contrasting
Italian inflection. 'For I think I know...can see...As I talk to
know exactly what I am...what I think...I see I treat you like
this?'

CHAPTER SEVEN

IT WAS downright amazing! Joanna decided astoundedly.
How he had somehow managed to turn everything on
its head like this! Just what did he think it was? she
wondered. A competition as to which of them had received the worst treatment? Did he think she *liked* doing
that to him? That she *liked* becoming that abominable
creature he had just described to her?

'All right!' she declared, facing up to him like a boxer
who had decided to come out of her corner and fight.
'You want the full and gory details, Sandro? OK, I'll
give them to you!'

And, leaning forward to brace her hands on the back
of one of his elegant lemon-drop sofas, she told him—
told him everything in a tight staccato voice that described in detail the whole wretched ordeal, from the
moment she'd found herself alone with those two men
to the moment when they'd walked away from her.

By the time she came to a shuddering halt she was
whiter than white, and Sandro had dropped into a nearby
chair where he had buried his face in his hands.

Then he was slowly sliding his hands away from his
face, though his dark head remained lowered, as if he
was unable to bring himself to look at her now the full
truth of it was out. It was like adding insult to injury,
considering he was the one who had insisted on all of
this.

Perhaps he was thinking something similar, because,
'I'm sorry,' he dropped with a dull thud into the drum-
ming silence. 'I should not have put you through that.
But I needed—'

'To know,' she finished for him when he stopped to swallow. 'If their "despoiling" of me was as brutal as my *emasculation* of you? Well, actually, it wasn't. They didn't even hurt me,' she informed him, hands rubbing up and down her ice-cold arms. 'I had no cuts,' she explained, 'no bruises. Nothing much at all to show that anything dire had ever actually happened. So I went home to Molly and said nothing,' she said. 'I went to work the next day and the next and the next...'

'Stop it now, Joanna, please,' Sandro inserted rawly.

But she couldn't stop—didn't want to stop. He had started the torrent, now it had to run its full course whether he wanted to listen or not.

'I dressed myself up in white for purity, and walked down the church aisle with you as the perfect virgin bride. I smiled for the cameras, for you, for Molly and your family. The hazy fog surrounding me only lifted when I found myself alone with you here in this apartment, and I looked at you and thought—My God! This man is expecting his bride to be a virgin! And, well...' She shrugged. 'You know the rest.'

Oh, yes, she confirmed silently, Sandro knew the rest. He had already described it with a raw and cutting honesty.

His life with a wife who had been utterly incapable of being a wife.

The day she left him she'd had visions of him going down on his knees to thank Heaven for deliverance from a marriage made in Hell; she had expected to feel the same way about the break-up herself!

But living without him had been worse than living with him—and living with him had been torment enough. She loved him and had missed him, even though the thought of going anywhere near him had brought her out in a cold sweat.

So—what now? she wondered. Where did all of this

wretched soul-baring leave them now that he knew it all?

Was he regretting his decision to begin their marriage again, now he knew exactly what he would be getting? Something was certainly troubling him because of the way he was sitting there, frowning at his own feet like that.

Panic flared—a new kind of panic, a panic that almost knocked her sideways, because it revolved around Sandro *not* wanting her now, rather than the other way round.

And this time, she told herself painfully, I really can't take any more.

'I'm sorry,' she choked, then turned and ran—out of the room, down the hallway and to the room she had been using before.

Once inside she closed the door behind her, then leaned back against it with a death grip on the door handle while she tried to snatch at a few short breaths of air in an effort to calm what was threatening to completely overwhelm her.

The fear of losing him—again.

Last time she had lost him because she couldn't tell him the truth; this time she was going to lose him because of the truth.

Her heart gave a painful lurch, her eyes deep, dark pools of utter despair. Then she glanced absently at the bed, saw the rumpled covers she had scrambled out of that morning, saw the breakfast tray lying on top of them, where she had left it untouched.

Quite suddenly it all closed right in on her, the hurt, the grief, the ugliness and misery, tunnelling down to that silly tray with its rack of cold toast and its pot of cold coffee.

Her hand snapped away from the door handle and she walked unsteadily forward. She came to a stop by the bed then bent, her eyes blurring out of focus, as trembling fingers picked up what she hadn't noticed lying on the tray that morning when Sandro had brought it to her.

It was a rose, a single red rose, with its stem cut short, its thorns removed and its bud just about ready to burst open.

He'd used to do this all the time, she recalled. An incurable romantic, who would bring her short-stemmed roses with their thorns removed so she would not prick herself. He'd used to lay them on the table at Vito's restaurant and wait until she decided to acknowledge that the rose had been placed there for her, his eyes mocking, hers wickedly teasing, because it was a game they played.

The lover waiting to be acknowledged as the lover. The loved making him wait, because it had heightened the wonderful electric tension between them until it fairly sizzled in the atmosphere as she went about her business, serving at other tables, and Sandro watched her do it with a lazy understanding of what was really going on.

Loving without touching. Knowing without words. A single short-stemmed rose that lay on a table making its own special statement, the link between the red-haired saucy waitress and the excruciatingly sophisticated, tall, dark Italian diner.

This latest rose floated across her trembling lips, its delicate scent filling her nostrils and closing her eyes, making her heart ache in bleak sad memory.

He had done the same kind of thing after they were married, too. Even in the midst of all the tension that surrounded them then, red roses would appear—by her plate at breakfast, on her pillow at night when she would crawl into her lonely bed in the room next to his.

Sandro's silent statement. Sandro's reminder that she was loved—still loved—no matter what she was doing to him.

Now here was another rose, making a statement when

statements were no longer valid, because he hadn't
known it all when he'd left the bloom for her this morning.

He hadn't known.

The floodgates opened quite without warning. Only
this time it wasn't bitter, ugly words that came flooding
out—but tears—tears she hadn't cried for years: tears of
misery, tears of anguish, tears of pain, grief, anger and
bitterness that had her sinking down onto the rumpled
bed and keeling sideways, where she curled herself into
a tight ball beside the tray with the rose clutched to her
breasts and just completely let go of it all.

Outside, down the hallway, through the half-open
door to the drawing room, Sandro stood by the window,
his fists rammed into his trouser pockets as he listened
to the dreadful storm without moving a muscle. His eyes
were fixed on some obscure point on the distant skyline,
his jaw locked solid, his teeth clenched behind grimly
pressed lips.

When it finally went quiet, he pulled his fists out of
his pockets and continued to stand there a few moments
longer, staring at the plaster still covering his grazed
knuckle, shifting his gaze to the other uninjured knuckle.
Then he grimaced, as if he were considering throwing
that fist at some solid object but knew it would be in-
sanity to do it.

He moved then, gave himself a mental shake and
walked into the hallway. Fifteen minutes after that he
was knocking on Joanna's bedroom door and pushing it
open, bringing the tempting aroma of a tomato-based
Italian sauce in with him.

'Lunch,' he announced. 'Five minutes, in the kitchen,
cara.'

Lunch, Joanna repeated silently as she watched the
door draw shut behind his retreating figure. The emotional holocaust was over, so it was back to normal.

The man must have emotions cased in steel, she decided bitterly.

Then she remembered the rose still clutched in her hand, and bitterness changed to a melting softness that threatened to bring the tears rushing back again.

She made herself join him for lunch, simply because she had had previous experience of what happened if she went against him; she knew what came next when Sandro used that coolly detached tone of voice.

But she refused to look at him, refused to so much as acknowledge his presence in the kitchen as she sat down at the table already laid out with steaming hot pasta topped with a delicious-smelling sauce.

'Help yourself,' he invited, sitting down opposite her.

Silently she did so, spooning a small amount from the dish onto her plate, then breaking off a chunk of warm bread while he watched her, saying nothing. Yet even his silence was critical.

He waited until she had forced the first forkful to her reluctant mouth and swallowed it before deciding to help himself, and every move he made, every perfectly normal gesture, played across her nerve-ends like static along live wire.

They sat through the whole meal like that: silent, tense—she forcing herself to eat because she did not want the sarcastic comments if she gave up on the first food she'd allowed into her stomach in more than twenty-four hours. And he, she suspected, was aware that her self-control was being held together by the merest thread which he did not want to snap.

And, to be fair, the food improved with each mouthful; Sandro was a surprisingly good cook. He enjoyed it, he'd told her once during one of those rare moments of harmony when they had been moving about his Belgravia kitchen preparing dinner together on his housekeeper's day off.

But those moments had been very few and far be-

tween. Most of the time there'd been this same tension
between them. Tension, tension, tension...

'What now?' she asked huskily when the silent meal
was finally over.

He glanced up, looking startled by her voice, as
though he had forgotten she was even there. Their eyes
clashed, then his became hooded again. She wasn't surprised; Sandro had not looked her directly in the face
once since she'd made her grand confession.

'I have to go to my office here for an hour or two,'
he said, with a quick glance at his watch. 'I suggest you
try to rest,' he advised. 'You look—wrung out.'

Washed out, wrung out and hung out to dry was probably more truthful. 'I mean...about this—situation...'
She made it clearer. 'I need to know what you intend to
do now.'

He leaned back in his chair, the action so graceful it
drew her eyes towards him, to his shirt-front, then to the
long, lean length of his upper torso.

The man with everything, she thought to herself, and
grimaced. Good looks, great body, loads of class and
style and sophistication. And, of course, there was that
other extra ingredient he possessed in abundance called
sex appeal.

The kind of sex appeal that few women were able to
resist. She'd seen it happen so many times—all he
needed to do was walk into a room full of people to
automatically become the centre of attention for every
female present.

Old and young alike; it didn't make any difference.
He possessed what Molly had used to call charisma—
that special quality which turned just a chosen few into
stars.

'Do?' he repeated, bringing her blue gaze fluttering
up towards his face, then instantly down and away from
it again. 'But I have just told you what I intend to do,'
he coolly informed her. 'I will spend the rest of today

attempting to clear my desk so I can keep tomorrow free for us to drive to Orvieto.'

Tomorrow—the beautiful villa in the brochure he had shown her; she had forgotten all about that! 'But I th-thought...' Her voice trailed off, her bewilderment so clear that Sandro sighed.

'Nothing has changed, *cara*,' he said. 'You are still my wife and I am still the man to whom you are married. This is still only the second day of this new life we are building, and, whatever transpires, you will remain my wife and I will remain your husband. You understand me?'

She understood only too well. She understood why relief was flooding through her right now—followed by the expected burst of alarm. But she also understood that he was reminding her of one very small but important point she seemed to have forgotten throughout all of this.

Mainly, that there was no way out for either of them. They had been married in accordance with the Roman Catholic faith, had made their vows to each other in front of God. Under Church law, that meant no going back, no matter how sour the marriage became. Therefore she was, in his eyes, his responsibility for life—for richer or poorer, for better or for worse.

Just another point of conflict for them to bite on, she concluded. Because when she'd let him marry her, knowing what she did, she had been playing him false.

'Y-you could get an annullment,' she suggested. 'I would support your claim if you wanted to go to the Church and ask for a release from your vows to me.'

'Well, thank you,' Sandro drawled, coming to his feet with a suddenness that spoke of anger. 'That is so very kind of you, *cara*, to allow me the pleasure of offering myself up for public ridicule by announcing to all and sundry that I have not been man enough to make love to my own wife!'

Joanna flushed at his sarcasm. 'I was only trying to be objective about the situation!' she snapped.

'Well, don't bother, if that is the only idea you can come up with,' he advised, then was suddenly leaning over her, one hand placed on the table, the other on the back of her chair, effectively trapping her, while his eyes made glinting contact with hers at last. 'Because you owe me, Joanna,' he informed her grimly. 'You owe me my pride, my self-respect, and my belief in myself as an acceptable member of the human race. None of that has changed simply because I now know *why* you treated me the way you did.'

'You want revenge,' she whispered in appalled understanding.

'I want—reparation,' he corrected.

'Oh, very Italian,' she mocked, turning her face away from him because looking at him hurt—hurt every which way she thought about it.

'No,' he muttered. And she wasn't sure what angered him the most, her turning away or her mockery, but suddenly he was taking hold of her chin and tugging it back round to face him. '*This* is very Italian!' he rasped.

Then his mouth was crushing her mouth with a kiss aimed to make a statement, a very angry sexual statement. It was ruthless and it was savage; he was parting her lips to deepen the kiss without any compunction.

She mumbled a protest and closed her eyes tightly shut, her body stiffening instinctively within the grip of his hands while she waited for the expected burst of panic to go rolling through her.

But it didn't come; instead she felt pleasure, a too long subdued, aching kind of pleasure that flared up from the very depths of her dark memories to rage in a pulse-singing rampage that had her lips parting and moving in hungry rhythm with his.

What's happening to me? she wondered deliriously. I should be fighting him like a lunatic. I *need* to fight him!

But she didn't fight him. Instead her hands flew up, clutching at his wide shoulders, then shifting in a hectic jerk to clasp him around the back of his neck. Her fingers tingled as they ran urgently into his hair, revelled in the muscles cording his nape as she drew him closer. She gave herself up to the intense pleasure she discovered in the warm, moist hollow of his hungry mouth.

Someone groaned, she wasn't certain who, but in another moment she was standing, her chair pushed out of the way and her body pressed against the full length of his. Sandro's hands were stroking her, moving in sensually urgent caresses from underarms to waist, then back up again, his thumbs brushing against the sides of her breasts. They responded by pulsing into tight, tingling life, ecstatic to join in with the whole wild conflagration.

She was on fire—that quickly and that violently—she was on fire for him, could hear his fractured breathing, could feel the fire burning through him, too, as he pressed himself even closer, letting her feel the strength of his desire, letting her know by the way he deepened the kiss even further that he was very aware of what was happening to her.

Then he was putting distance between them, prising his mouth from hers to hold her at arm's length while his eyes spat a bloody kind of anger at her and his kiss-swollen mouth pulsed with an undisguised passion.

'Well, that was a revelation,' he mocked with silken cruelty.

But she was much too shocked to appreciate the mockery. She just stared at him, dazed and shaken, still lost within her own stunningly passionate response to what had begun as a punishment and ended up as the most intensely erotic kiss she had ever—ever experienced.

'Keep this up, *mi amore*,' he continued in that same

taunting vein, 'and reparation is going to be well worth the years I have waited to get it!'

She flinched, his cruelty finally managing to get through the haze. 'I can't bear this,' she breathed in stark confusion.

'Correction,' he clipped. 'You are bearing it very well, if my senses are telling me the real truth of it.'

And, to punctuate the humiliating point, he kissed her again, capturing her mouth but waiting only long enough for her lips to cling helplessly to his before he brutally separated them again.

'See what I mean, *cara*?' he drawled. 'You want me so badly you cannot hide it any longer.'

Letting go of her altogether, he watched her sway dizzily, her long lashes fluttering dazedly over her darkened blue eyes.

Then, drily, he remarked, 'Tonight should be interesting.' On that strategically-placed barb he strode coolly for the door, tossing casually over his shoulder, 'And just in case you consider trying it,' he warned, 'the lift will not be operational to this floor until I return. So don't start any fires, *cara*—not while I am away at least.'

And with that he was gone, leaving her with that tasty little tit-bit to chew over.

Tonight, he had said—and said it calculatingly. Which, in turn, could only mean one thing.

Weakly she sank back into the chair. It was all getting worse by the minute.

It didn't matter one bit to him that she had just bared her very soul to him. He wanted reparation and he was determined to get it. And reparation could only come in one form as far as he was concerned.

Sandro fully intended to make their marriage a real one tonight.

Consequently she was in a state of high anxiety by the time he returned that evening. Out of sheer desperation she had kept herself busy throughout the afternoon—clearing their lunch away, tidying her bed but refusing to so much as take a step towards the other bedroom Sandro had used the last time she had been here. Then she went to search out something to cook for dinner, something mind-consuming enough to stop her driving herself into hysterics at the terrible sense of helplessness that was just too familiar to her to deal sensibly with it.

It didn't matter that she knew without a doubt Sandro would never, ever use force on her; that awful feeling of utter helplessness still ate away at her nerves as she stood rolling gnocchi—tiny bite-sized potato dumplings—and prepared her own fresh pasta—all learned during her time at Vito's restaurant. She could cook French food too, and English, of course, and she wasn't too bad with Chinese dishes—again picked up during various restaurant jobs.

But this was an Italian man's kitchen, so the ingredients in it were mainly Italian. So gnocchi it would be for starters, dropped into a rich, hot butter sauce and followed by a pasta bake, packed with mushrooms, onions and peppers in a creamy sauce and topped with mozzarella cheese.

'Mmm,' a light voice said. 'This all looks and smells very wifely.'

Joanna spun round from the sauce she was grimly stirring. 'I am not sleeping with you tonight, Sandro!' she told him shrilly.

She looked hot, she looked bothered, she looked just about ready to fall apart at the seams. She had tied her hair back in an unattractive tight knot on the top of her head, and she had changed out of the jeans and dragged on the most unflattering items of clothing she could find in the wardrobe: white wide-legged trousers and a long black jumper that was suffocating her in the heat permeating the kitchen.

He, by contrast, looked cool and at ease and as usual,

very stylish, even though the jacket to his suit had gone, along with his tie, and the cuffs of his shirt sleeves had been unbuttoned and left to hang loose about his strong brown wrists.

'What are you making?' He walked forward, ignoring what she'd said to him. 'Gnocchi?' he quizzed, glancing over her shoulder to see the tiny dumplings gently simmering in a pan on the cooker. 'I married an Englishwoman with an Italian heart!'

'I won't sleep with you,' she repeated, turning back to the sauce she had been working on when he came in.

'Shall I find some wine to go with this, or have you already done it?'

'No wine,' she snapped, 'I don't want wine—I want you to listen to me!'

'That pan is non-stick, *cara*,' he pointed out gently. 'You will take its protective coating off if you stir it as violently as that. I'll go and find a bottle of white, in case you change your mind later...'

He moved off; she spun again. 'Sandro!' she called after him, and it was a wretched cry from the heart.

It stopped him, but he didn't turn. 'I am not listening to you, Joanna,' he informed her flatly. 'It is time to come to terms with what happened to you. Three years of your life is quite long enough to devote to the experience.' Then, *'Mamma mia!'* he added with tragic Latin drama as he continued walking. 'It is more than long enough!'

'You're so damned insensitive!' she sobbed furiously after him. 'I hate you! If you so much as touch me my skin will shrivel!'

He didn't even bother to answer that one, disappearing into a utility room off the kitchen, which led through to his impressively well-stocked wine cellar, leaving her standing there feeling bitten through to her very centre with a helpless, anguished frustration. It wasn't fair! she thought tragically. She had taken enough—more than enough—over the last two days, yet still he wouldn't listen to reason!

A tear tried to roll down her cheek but she angrily swiped it away, going back to her sauce as if her life depended on it. He came back with a bottle of wine, found an ice bucket and emptied a tray of cubes into it before adding the bottle. From her station by the stove Joanna grimly ignored him, while every single sensor she possessed was on full alert to pick up exactly what he was doing and where he was doing it as he moved around the hot kitchen.

'How long?' he asked.

'Tw—twenty minutes.'

'Then you have time to get a quick shower and change,' he opined. 'You can safely leave the rest to me.'

'I don't—'

'Don't argue, Joanna,' he interrupted, coming to stand behind her and taking the spoon right out of her hand. 'You are hot,' he stated, turning her round to face him, 'you are uptight, and you are not going to close that door on me again,' he added determinedly. 'So, be sensible and go and make yourself comfortable before we sit down to eat. You know I am not going to hurt you in any way, *amore*,' he tagged on gently. 'At least let your common sense tell you that.'

She sniffed, her unhappy face bowed, unable to let her common sense tell her anything while he was standing so close. His sleeve-cuffs were still dangling, she noticed inconsequently, which made them dangerous around a hot cooker. Automatically she reached out to fold one up his arm for him. He didn't say a word but let her tidy him, even holding out the other arm when she'd finished with the first, so she could see to that too.

'You can't possibly begin to understand how I'm feeling right now,' she said shakily.

'Then explain it to me.'

But she shook her head, watching his gold Rolex watch appear as she folded back the white cuff of his shirt, seeing brown skin and dark hair, strong muscle and sinew.

She could also picture this man naked, walking towards her, his eyes so black she could see the twin fires of a powerful desire burning brightly behind them.

Sucking in a sharp, shaken gulp of air, she moved around him, away from him, out of the room at the speed of light, that vision one she had not seen in a long time— and it scared her as much now as it had done when it actually happened. Here, in this apartment, in his bedroom, on their wedding night.

He'd been right about the shower and the change of clothes; she did feel more comfortable, though no less uptight, when she went back to find that Sandro had set the table in the small dining room just off the kitchen. Like all of his homes, this apartment had two sides to it: its homely side and its formal side. One set of rooms devoted entirely to personal creature comforts, the other for entertaining on a grand scale.

Not that she had ever been present when Sandro had entertained like that, she remembered heavily. She had been too shot through with insecurities for him to dare expose himself to the embarrassment of showing off his neurotic wife.

So they'd spent most of their year living together more or less isolated from other people—except for Molly, of course, who had lived with them for the first six months.

'Here, take these,' Sandro said as she walked into the kitchen. He was holding out two warm plates wrapped in a linen teatowel. 'I want to open the wine before I bring it in...'

All very normal, she noted. Very let's-pretend-everything-is-fine! Tight-lipped, she took the plates from him and carried them into the small dining room. She found he'd lit candles and wanted to smash the damn china over his head!

Which meant the tension between them had the same effect as nettle rash as they sat down together to eat.

'Pretty dress,' he remarked, long lashes sweeping down over his eyes as he took in the simple but classical lines of the royal-blue silk shift dress she had chosen to wear.

'You should know; you bought it,' she tossed deflatingly back.

'From now on you will dress as I want you to dress,' he smoothly declared. 'It is part of your therapy that you will dress up to your beauty and not down to your low opinion of yourself.'

There didn't seem to be any answer to that so she didn't try to look for one, because he was only telling it how it was. She did dress down, but she always had done; it wasn't something that had developed because of what had happened to her. She'd always had an aversion to pandering to vanity—perhaps because that was what her mother had done. Until she became ill, her mother's life had revolved around how to get the best from herself. It had never seemed to occur to her that she was naturally pretty; she'd felt she had to work at it constantly, to the point where more often than not she'd gone right over the top.

Not that Sandro was likely to dress *her* in over-the-top garments, because his own sense of good taste just would not let him.

'What's happened to your housekeeper?' she asked in a clear change of subject. 'She hasn't been near the place today, as far as I can tell.'

'I've given her the next couple of weeks off,' he explained, pouring a bone-dry Chianti into lead crystal wine glasses. 'I thought we could do with the privacy while we get used to each other again.'

Privacy so he could keep the pressure on her, Joanna

corrected silently. She might be neurotic but she wasn't a fool; she knew he was still a man on a mission.

Which effectively ruined any hopes of them sharing this meal with any more harmony than they had shared during lunch. By the time it was over she felt so damned uptight that when Sandro climbed to his feet she almost jumped out of her wits.

'I will go and get my shower and change now, if you don't mind,' he said coolly, ignoring her reaction.

'Fine,' she said, coming to her feet herself. 'I'll just clear up here, then I think I'll go to bed,' she told him stiffly. 'I'm very tired...'

Hint—big hint. She expected another argument; she expected him to order her to stay right where she was until he got back.

But, 'Suit yourself,' was all he said as he walked away. 'I'll use another room so I won't disturb you.'

Another room. Joanna wilted in sinking relief, only to come upright again almost immediately when it suddenly occurred to her that he was behaving out of character by saying that!

What was he up to? she wondered as she cleared away the dinner things. Why ease the pressure now, after piling it on so steadily throughout the long day?

Well, there was one thing for sure, she decided: she wasn't hanging around to find out!

So she was shut safely in her room and curled up in bed by the time she heard him come out of that other bedroom further down the hallway.

He didn't even pause to listen at her closed door as he passed by it.

She frowned, not understanding him—not understanding him one little bit! She didn't understand herself either, because there was something niggling at her insides that felt very much like disappointment.

She fell asleep like that, still niggled, still tense,

clutching a spare pillow to her front as if it were a magic charm that could ward off any unwanted callers.

Yet, if that was its function, it didn't work. The unwanted callers came in her dreams. She supposed she should have expected it after what she'd been through over the last couple of days. As it was, she woke up sweating, gasping for breath in the darkened bedroom, frightened and disorientated for the few fevered seconds it took her to remember where she was. Then she just lay there, waiting for it all to fade away again.

But it didn't fade away, and she knew she was going to have to get up and out of here while she gave herself time to get over the whole horror.

She was just about to slide out of the bed when her hand touched something very warm and alive lying next to her, and all of a sudden everything inside her went haywire, shooting her into a sitting position as her mouth opened wide and she let loose an ear-piercing scream.

It brought Sandro awake with a start that had him sitting up too, before he had even opened his eyes. 'What the hell—?' he gasped.

CHAPTER EIGHT

'OH,' JOANNA whispered in quivering relief. 'It's you.'

'Who the hell else would be sleeping next to you?' Sandro rasped, so angry that she realised he was responding to her shock, not her comments.

'Bad dream,' she breathed in an attempted explanation.

'Ah,' he said, for once sounding the disconcerted one. Then, more gently, 'Are you OK?'

She shook her head, fighting not to suffocate in air that, to her, reeked of the stench of stale beer and male body odour. It was amazing how the subconscious mind could be so brutally authentic when it wanted to torture you.

'I can't stay here,' she said, and scrambled out of bed to drag on her robe. She hurried from the room without even bothering to ask what he was doing in her bed! It didn't seem that important when other far more dreadful horrors were having a field day in her mind.

The rest of the apartment was in darkness, the quietness in itself almost as suffocating as the room she had just left. Still trembling in the aftermath, she made for the drawing room, her bare feet moving silently on cool mosaic flooring as she walked down the hall and pushed open the drawing room door.

It was dark in there, too; her hand lifted, fumbling along the wall beside the door in search of a light switch. The room came alive with a clever burst of subdued lighting from several strategically placed table lamps,

Still shaking, she moved across to a lemon sofa and

134

curled herself into one corner while she waited for her
skin to stop crawling and her heart to stop hammering.

Yet the dream had not been as bad as it could have
been. In the beginning—after she'd finally left Sandro
and was living with Molly, which was when the dreams
had first begun—she'd used to wake up screaming so
hysterically that it used to frighten poor Molly out of
her wits!

Much as she had just done to Sandro, she realised,
frowning because it was just beginning to sink in that
he had been in bed with her.

He came into the drawing room then, dressed in a
hastily knotted short black cotton robe that did nothing
to dampen his masculinity. 'What happened back there?'
he demanded, the coils of sleep still showing around the
lazy fringes of his eyes.

'I told you. Bad dream. What were you doing in my
bed?' she countered.

Yawning, he threw himself into a chair opposite her.
'Where you sleep, I sleep,' he answered simply. 'It is
what husbands and wives do.'

Well, not this husband and wife, Joanna thought. 'You
said you would use another room,' she reminded him.

'To shower,' he clarified, yawned again, then had the
gall to begin to fall back to sleep as he lounged in the
chair!

'Go away, Sandro,' she snapped, more to wake him
up than to give him his marching orders. 'I'll be OK
here on my own.'

Then she frowned again, because she'd suddenly remembered that she used to say the very same thing to
Molly. Go away, I'll be OK. But she never was OK, was
she? She used to shiver and shake, much as she was
doing now, and poor Molly would hover anxiously, not
knowing how to react.

Oh, Molly, she thought, and tipped back her head to
sigh heavily as she closed her weary eyes. Why did all

of this have to happen? Why did you have to die, and why did I have to end up being like this?'

'Joanna...'

'Shh,' she said. 'I'm busy missing Molly.'

Strange thing to say, yet he seemed to understand because he got up, ran a tired hand through his tumbled hair, then said quietly, 'What about a warm drink?'

'Mmm,' she accepted, 'that sounds nice.' Mainly because it was easier than saying no.

He left the room and she went back to thinking about her sister. Poor Molly had worried so much about her, she remembered. The way she'd lived, like a lifeless zombie, the way she'd snapped if Molly tried to ask questions. And the way the dreams had used to come and scare the living daylights out of both of them. So much so that in the end, she'd felt compelled to give Molly some explanation, because her sister had been ready to put all of the blame onto Sandro.

By then Molly had her own little flat, not far from the London college she'd been studying at. It had been a kind of compromise in the end, that Molly would continue her studies so long as Joanna—with Sandro's financial help—would let her live near the campus.

Her marriage had fallen into such dire straits by then that she had actually been glad to get her sister out of Sandro's home, because then they could at least be open about all the stress between them, instead of having to pretend nothing was the matter for Molly's sake.

Or maybe Molly had felt the tension anyway and had been relieved to get away from it, Joanna grimly suggested to herself. She wouldn't have blamed Molly if that was the truth of it; those first few months of her marriage had been absolutely dreadful, with Sandro insisting that they share a bed even though she spent the whole night clinging to the edge of the mattress so she wouldn't turn over and cling to him instead.

But once Molly moved out, so Joanna moved out—of his bedroom.

Now it seemed that that situation had gone into a complete reversal. She was back living with Sandro, and he was back sharing her bed.

He returned with two steaming cappuccinos liberally sprinkled with cocoa. He put them down on the coffee table but instead of going back to his own chair sat himself down right in next to her, so the firmness of his hips pressed against the curve of her stomach. Smiling down at her, he lifted a hand to gently remove a red-gold skein of hair from her cheek, then kissed her.

She didn't flinch, wasn't even close to flinching because the kiss was so openly passive.

'Feeling better?' he asked.

She nodded. 'Sorry if I frightened you,' she added.

'Don't mention it,' he murmured. 'Would you like to talk about it?'

'If I say no will you start bullying me?' she countered wryly.

'No.' His reply was deep and sincere, and it did things to her insides she found very confusingly nice. 'I find that even I am not quite that ruthless,' he admitted with a small wry grimace.

'You are ruthless enough to sleep in my bed uninvited,' Joanna pointed out.

'That's different,' he said. 'And anyway, you never even noticed me getting in it, so what are you complaining about?'

'I wasn't complaining,' she argued. 'I was merely making a protest.'

'No, you were not,' he smiled, still gently stroking that now very tidy coil of hair round her earlobe. 'You were searching for an excuse so you could let me stay there without you having to kick up a fuss.'

'What a lie!' she objected.

'Is it?' he quizzed. 'Then, what if I promise to keep

the bad dreams away if you let me stay in your bed? Will that do?'

It was stupid, she knew, but his gentle teasing caused tears to suddenly bulged in her eyes.

'Ah, don't do that, *cara*,' Sandro pleaded unsteadily. 'It cut me up enough hearing you weep this morning.'

'You never even noticed,' she choked out accusingly.

'See this fist?' he demanded, showing her the one with the plaster that still covered the bruising. 'It almost had a matching one.'

It was pure impulse that made Joanna reach out with both hands to draw his uninjured fist to her cheek for safe-keeping. It moved him; that one simple gesture seemed to move him so deeply that her tears came back all over again.

Why? Because even she realised it was the first time she had voluntarily reached out and touched him like that in so long. It was wretched.

'Come on.' He sounded suddenly unlike himself. 'I'm taking you back to bed,' he said, gathering her into his arms and standing up with her, 'where I am going to hold you close for the rest of the night. And if you argue I am going to kiss you senseless. That's the deal, *cara*,' he stated firmly, not seeming to have noticed that she wasn't arguing. 'Sleeping, or kissing.'

'No bartering. No haggling?' she said drily.

He grinned. 'You want to haggle? I should warn you first that I am very good. It is the banker in me. I can haggle the pants off the best of them,'

Wrong choice of words, perhaps, but Joanna chose to ignore them. She was too tired, for one thing. But mainly she was simply too weary of running for cover all the time. Perhaps Sandro was right, she mused sleepily as he lowered her feet to the floor by the bed so he could deal with her robe before urging her back into the bed.

He joined her in seconds, removing his own robe to reveal a pair of loose white boxer shorts that did little to disguise his masculinity. Yet she didn't feel threatened, felt no desire to pull away from him when he collected her unresisting body to his.

Maybe he was right: the more he touched her, the more she would grow to accept it. Maybe the baring of her darkest secrets this morning had exorcised the ghosts. Maybe they really did have a chance at making a go of this, after all...

She could not have been more wrong about anything she discovered the next morning.

Joanna awoke at dawn to the sound of a bird singing on the ledge outside the window and lay listening to it for ages before eventually rolling over with the intention of drifting back to sleep again.

It was then and only then, as she found herself staring into his face, that she remembered.

Almost instantly the alarm bells began to ring inside her, then died away again when she realised he was still fast asleep, with a strong brown arm thrown across the pillow just above her resting head.

She went still, relaxing into the mattress while she indulged herself in the rare luxury of looking at him without having to worry about doing it.

He was, she acknowledged, as beautiful in sleep as he was awake, and stimulatingly vital. So dark, so feature-perfect, so lean and tight—that impressive torso of his shamelessly naked so she could lie here and feast on firm chest muscles densely dusted by a layer of springy black hair. Feast on this man who, for some reason she had never been able to understand, had wanted this little waitress when he could have had anyone.

It had been his misfortune, she thought sadly. Because—look at him, she told herself: tall, dark and handsome as he was, strong, stubborn and determined as he was. And even though he had carried her back here to this bed, and virtually coiled himself around her, there

was not a single point at which their bodies brushed
now,

Why? she asked herself with an aching sadness that
stemmed directly from guilt. Because she knew that he
had become so well conditioned during their marriage
not to let himself come close to her. Even while he slept
he was still maintaining that maxim now, in his subconscious.

A sigh whispered from her, the kind that told her she
should be thinking of sliding out of this bed before
Sandro woke up and yet another round of mental torment
would begin as he probed what she was thinking and
feeling about this situation when she just didn't know
how she felt about it. She was confused—extremely confused.

I love you, Alessandro, she whispered with a melan-
choly softness inside her head. I'm sorry for everything
I've ever done to you.

She might as well have shouted the words at him because his dark lashes suddenly fluttered away from his
eyes, catching her exposed and vulnerable, catching her
with nowhere to run and hide.

He didn't move, he didn't speak, and neither did she.
Their eyes caught in that one long knowing moment as
everything that had ever gone before it flooded painfully
through her then ebbed away.

'What time is it?' she asked, because she felt the need
to say something and that was all she could come up
with just then.

His long, lush lashes lifted higher, revealing yet more
of those rich, dark, slumberous eyes as he glanced at the
silk-draped window through which a golden dawn was
seeping softly into the room.

'Around five at a guess,' he judged, then the eyes were
back on her again. 'You had a bad dream last night,' he
seemed compelled to remind her.

She nodded. 'I remember.'

Another silence fell between them. Not tense, for a change, but wary. Because that barrier of space still lay between them? she wondered. Neither of them had moved so much as a finger or toe since he'd opened his eyes. She was afraid to, too frightened of beginning what she sensed was only just staying hidden beneath the surface of all this uncanny stillness.

'It's still early,' he murmured. 'Go back to sleep. We have a couple more hours left before we need to think about moving from here...'

Sleep, she repeated to herself as she watched his eyes close, watched those lashes lower over rich brown irises then settle against his satin-smooth cheekbones.

Sleep, when her hands wanted to reach out and stroke him, when her lips wanted to taste that warm, dark skin.

Sleep, where she would only dream of him, instead of lying here being able to look at the real thing.

No, she didn't want to sleep. She wanted to stay wide awake and hoard the moment, gather it up and hold it close as she always did with her special moments with this special man.

Then, that strong brown arm above her head moved—not much—but the corded muscles flexed a little and she was instantly aware of the defensive tensing of her own muscles in response.

His eyes flicked open as if he sensed the very moment when all the old anxieties came bubbling up inside her. Anger sparked in their dark brown depths, and she didn't blame him for letting it because he hadn't even touched her! Hadn't so much as accidentally brushed a single hair on her head!

'I'm sorry,' she jerked out anxiously.

'Too damned late,' he bit back, and suddenly he was most definitely touching her, his naked upper torso rolling across her, hot and hard, pressing her into the mattress, big arms curving about her head so his hands could frame her anxious face. 'One day soon,' he muttered, 'I am going to drag you out from behind your insecurities and lay you out naked in front of me! Then I am going to devour you, *cara mia*! I am going to eat every single last morsel of you and not even bother to spit out the bones!'

'I said I was sorry!' she cried. 'I didn't mean to do it! I was just—' Engrossed in looking at you, she had been going to say, but stopped herself.

So Sandro put his own biting conclusion to her cut-off sentence. 'Reacting predictably!'

'No!' she denied. 'I was startled, that was all!'

He didn't believe her. 'Prove it,' he said. 'If you were only "startled".' He mocked the word deridingly and moved against her, his forearms taking most of his weight, though there was enough of it for her to feel completely overwhelmed by the man. 'Prove it,' he repeated challengingly. 'And convince me you were not about to run screaming for cover.'

Her heart began to hammer. This situation was quickly racing out of control. She began to wish she *had* run screaming for cover, had taken her chance when she'd had it earlier and just got the hell out of this bed before Sandro even opened his eyes!

'I don't know what it is you expect me to do to prove something that was sheer reflex!' she snapped out irritably.

'Well…' he drawled, and suddenly he was no longer angry but lazily sardonic, a much more dangerous mood when she found herself trapped beneath him. 'You could try another reflex reaction, and put your arms around my neck, then pull me down so you could kiss me.'

'I don't want to kiss you.' She stiffly rebuffed the suggestion.

'Why not?' he asked. 'You were dying to kiss me a few moments ago,' he taunted provokingly.

Her eyes flashed with comprehension. 'You were

watching me look at you!' she accused him in mortified horror.

'Mmm,' he admitted with a lazy smugness. 'I found it most arousing to have your eyes caress my body like that.'

She shut those stupid eyes, wishing herself a million miles away from here now, and tried to move out from beneath him. Only to go perfectly still when the movement made her so intensely aware of his long, lean, warm nakedness that her cheeks bloomed with heat— the same heat that began running along her veins in a helter-skelter ride of wild exhilaration.

'Are you going to kiss me?'

She shook her head, keeping her eyes tightly shut while her breasts heaved against his resting chest, and her abdomen began to curl with tension.

Did he know what was happening to her? She was sure he knew, because of the way he laid his next silken challenge before her. 'You would prefer it if I moved away from you?' he suggested. 'Give you back your own space?'

Her hands snapped up of their own volition, anchoring themselves around his neck. Sandro laughed, all male, all sexually confident male.

'You will understand, *mi amore*,' he continued in that same tormenting vein, 'that when I insist that you must kiss me, it is only because I have no wish to be accused of coercing you in any way.'

And this wasn't coercion? Having a full-blooded half-naked male resting sensually against her was not a terrible coercion in itself? Having these strong brown arms enclosing her, and that beautifully muscled torso pressing down on her, and one of those powerful thighs of his hooked across her own was just about the worst coercion she had ever experienced.

Then one of his hands gently cupped her breast and she went into emotional overload, groaning out a protest that was more a whimper of surrender as her spine arched and her hand applied the necessary pressure to bring his waiting mouth crushing down on her own.

In seconds her senses were raging wildly again. She seemed to have no control over them any longer! Her hands were doing exactly what *they* wanted to do, caressing his warm dark skin; her lips were doing what *they* were desperate to do, greedily tasting him, tasting him everywhere, anywhere she could place her hungry mouth to taste him.

'Joanna, this is too fast,' Sandro muttered in a thickened rasp as she literally caught fire beneath him.

And he was no longer taunting. He was no longer playing the sexually confident male who had just threatened to completely devour her. He was trying to subdue her, trying to stem the wild storm.

'Joanna…'

She caught his mouth in a kiss that devoured him instead, one hand clasped around his nape while the other ran in a feverish sweep down the full length of his back. He arched like a man shot by an arrow, groaned something painful, then just gave himself up to the whole bubbling turmoil, taking over, becoming the hot, hungry and passionate lover she had always known lurked beneath his impossible self-control.

As his touch grew bolder, caressing her where she'd never allowed him to caress her before, she thought elatedly, I can do this! I can actually let this happen now!

Only to feel the whole thing flip over like a spinning coin that falls to the ground to land the wrong way up. Suddenly the panic was back, sizzling along her veins and making her fight instead of encourage. She let out a choked whimper, then was pushing violently away from him, scrambling from the bed, standing swaying dizzily beside it, legs shaking, pulses frantic, her whole mind gone into a complete mental meltdown while Sandro remained where she had pushed him, watching it all happen with a kind of grimly rueful familiarity that almost tore her apart as much as her own sense of failure was managing to do.

He should have been angry, she would have preferred it if he'd got angry! But all he did, after watching her battle with herself for a while, was roll onto his back and drawl lazily, 'Well, at least that got a whole lot further than it ever did before. Things could well be looking up for us, *cara.*'

On a choke of distress she ran from the room.

The hour long drive to Orvieto along the main road out of Rome was accomplished in the most appalling tension—hers, not Sandro's. He, by comparison, seemed incredibly relaxed which, considering the way she had left him in a fierce state of physical arousal, was more distressing to her than the very unpalatable fact that she had been in no lesser state herself.

Yet, when she had eventually forced herself out of their bedroom—having had to wait until he'd decided to vacate it before she would go back in there to shower in the en suite bathroom, and get herself dressed and ready to face another day of pressure Sandro had planned for her—there he'd been, sitting at the table on the sunny breakfast terrace, reached via the small dining room, drinking coffee while he skimmed through a morning newspaper and looking just about as relaxed as anyone could look!

It was amazing. The man definitely had his emotions encased in steel, she'd decided. He had showered, shaved, and was wearing oatmeal-coloured trousers held up by a brown leather belt, and a plain white tee shirt was tucked in at his spare waist. As usual, he shrieked style, even though there was no obvious evidence of his clothes being anything special.

But there it was, Sandro in a nutshell: a man whose style came from within, but which was always evident.

'Help yourself,' he'd invited, indicating towards the coffee pot that had stood on the table next to a basket of warm bread rolls. 'We should try to leave here within the next hour,' he'd said smoothly. 'But you have time to eat and drink something before we go.'

She'd said nothing. What could she have said except, Why don't you put us both out of our misery and let me go again?

Then she'd seen it, tucked in beside her plate, and her eyes had filled with the now too-ready tears, her wretched mouth beginning to quiver. 'Sandro...' she'd whispered hoarsely.

'Shush,' he'd said, getting up from the table, then bending down to brush a kiss across her pale cheek. 'Enjoy your breakfast. I have to make a few phone calls before we leave.'

She'd watched him stride back into the apartment, leaving her sitting there feeling wretched, feeling hopeless, feeling utterly, heart-wrenchingly useless, as her fingers gently stroked along the thornless column of the short-stemmed red rose he had placed there for her.

I don't deserve him, she'd told herself—something she had always, always known.

By the time he'd come back for her the rose had disappeared, having been carefully folded into a napkin and placed inside her purse for future filing with her precious store of memorabilia. If she ever saw that store again, because she knew she would never ask Sandro for it. That would open up too many cans of wriggling worms that still had to be let loose.

'Ready?'

She'd nodded and stood up to join him, lifting very guarded eyes to his. But Sandro hadn't been looking into her face, he'd been too busy checking out what she was wearing, his dark eyes inspecting the cream linen trousers and the tiny cotton top of the same colour. She had managed to get her long hair to plait into a single braid

that swung between her shoulderblades this morning.
She wore no make-up. It was just too hot. So she had
applied some protective cream from the very expen-
sive-looking jar she had found in the bathroom.

Now she wished she'd piled on the make-up, because
at least it would have hidden the strained pallor that was
back in her face.

Together they had walked through the apartment and
out into the upper foyer, where he'd paused hesitantly,
then turned towards her. 'We can go down by the rear
fire escape, if you would prefer it,'

It had been a concession she'd felt neither pleased
about or grateful for, because it had only highlighted
what a pathetic waste of time she was.

'The lift is fine,' she'd said coolly and, to prove the
point, had stepped up to press the call button herself.
Personally, she'd been quietly impressed with the way
she'd stood calmly beside him while the lift took them
to ground level.

Sandro hadn't said a word, but what he had done was
reach for her hand and raise it to his mouth in a silent
praise as they'd waited for the doors to open. And even
that small gesture had only managed to make her feel
worse, because what had she done except overcome a
silly obsession she should have combated years ago?

That was why she was tense—that was why she was
silent and withdrawn and very uncommunicative. She
was cross with herself because living with her was like
living in a minefield—you never knew where the next
explosion of panic was going to come from!

She couldn't, in all fairness, put Sandro through that
kind of madness a second time. He had to learn that it
just wasn't worth the effort he was trying to put into it,
and the best way to do that was completely freeze him
out again.

She could do it, she told herself grimly. She had done
it very successfully once before, hadn't she?

CHAPTER NINE

ORVIETO lay about halfway between Rome and Siena on the Umbrian-Tuscany borders. It was an area of breathtaking beauty, with lush and fertile rolling hillsides covered by row upon row of vine trees broken by thick clusters of woodland. Enchanting old towns capped incredible hilltops which seemed to rise out of the ground for no apparent reason.

Yet, picturesque as the area was, it was so obviously intrinsically rural that she began to wonder what it was here that had caught Sandro's usually very urban eye.

'The estate is just over the next hillside,' Sandro said beside her. 'Look now,' he directed.

Her gaze drifted outwards, then simply stilled while she stared open-mouthed at the lovely valley that came into view. Despite her resolve, she responded, 'Oh, Sandro!' with a gasp of unrestrained pleasure. 'This is lovely! How much of it belongs to you?'

'To us,' he smoothly corrected. Then, before she could react to that stunning correction, 'As far as you can see,' he answered her question, bringing a further gasp escaping from her parted lips.

He turned the car then, steering them in through a gap in the rows of vine trees. It was a private driveway, columned on either side by tall cypresses that led them towards the pretty villa she recognised from the brochure Sandro had shown her the day before.

As they came closer to the house itself the vines began to give way to thick fruit orchards, then the most beautiful gardens set in typically formal Italian style with terraces already blooming with well-behaved colour.

148

It was, Joanna decided, the most beautiful place she had ever laid eyes on, the house itself looking as though it had sat there for ever, with its red-tiled roof and its yellowing walls basking in the golden sunlight.

Sandro pulled the car to a stop on a tiny cobbled area just in front of the house. Off to one side, Joanna could see what she recognised as the stable block—again looking as if it had always been there. Behind that stood tall, narrow cypress trees, acting like windbreaks or more probably as a boundary line, planted to separate the private accommodation from the working estate.

Joanna climbed out of the car and stood gazing around her, too captivated to maintain the indifference she had been so determined upon.

'Well?' Sandro murmured quietly from the other side of the car. 'What do you think?'

Think? She couldn't think; this place was just too enchanting for her to be able to think. Feel, maybe; she could feel many things: pleasure, wonder, a yearning desire to belong to this lovely place.

'Who in their right mind would want to sell this?' she asked rather breathlessly.

'The owner's daughter married a Californian wine-grower,' Sandro explained, coming around the car to stand beside her. 'They wanted to be close to her, so they put this place up for sale and moved to California. An expedient move on their side,' he added sagely. 'For this place may look picture-perfect but in fact it needs a lot of money spending on it to bring it up to New World standards in wine-growing and processing if it is going to compete.'

'And you fancied taking on the challenge?' Joanna began to understand at last. This was Sandro being Sandro, seeing a good investment.

But he thoroughly shocked her by saying quietly, 'I did not buy this for the challenge, Joanna. I bought it for you.'

For her? Her eyes whipped around to stare at him in open-mouthed disbelief. 'But why me?' she asked in bewilderment.

He didn't answer, just smiled a rather odd smile and said, 'Come on. We may as well inspect the house first.'

Then he was striding off towards the house, leaving her to follow more slowly, with her mind thrown back into clamouring confusion because never, not once, had she ever voiced a desire to live somewhere like this!

So, what was he playing at with his clever wordgames? she wondered frowningly. Then, reparation, she remembered, as she followed him into a large, cool entrance hall darkened by the wooden shutters pulled across the windows. Sandro was most definitely still a man on a mission, and that mission included reparation.

'The house requires some renovation,' he said, as she came to an uncertain halt just inside the open doorway. 'But nothing too drastic...'

He was already moving to open the shutters, throwing them back from the long narrow windows to allow light to come streaming in, dust motes dancing in the sunbeams onto disappointingly bare stone floors, plain white walls and a huge rustic fireplace. There was a spiral stairway leading up from a central situation against the far wall and several closed doors flanking either side of it.

But that seemed to be all. 'It's empty.' She voiced the absolute obvious.

'*Si,*' he acknowledged. 'Which is going to give you a lot to think about as you plan the refurbishing of the whole house.'

Joanna didn't answer. Her mind was boggling, her natural defensive system grinding into full action simply because she did not understand what was going on here. Yesterday he had implied that they were coming here to start their marriage properly, which meant sex, of course. But to enjoy the kind of sex Sandro had to be thinking about, there first had to be a bed, and this place did not look as if it had one stick of furniture anywhere in it.

In a daze, she moved off towards the nearest door and pushed it open to find yet another empty room darkened by wooden shutters covering the windows. 'What was this?' she enquired as he came up behind her.

His hands slid around her waist, long fingers easily spanning her. Sensation whipped like electrically charged wire in a tight coil around her whole body, and it took every ounce of self-control she possessed not to jump away from him like a severely scalded cat.

'A sitting room,' he replied. 'There are two of them—one either side of the front door...'

She nodded, unable to say another word, while he was still holding her. She didn't even dare breathe in case Sandro realised just how desperately aware she was of him.

'Shall I throw open the shutters?'

'Please,' she said, and almost wilted with relief as his hands left her so he could move past her and throw the room into dust-dancing light.

After that, she was careful to keep her distance from him as they walked from room to room, throwing open shutters and staring round the empty spaces while he described to her what they had been used for by the last owners.

The house was big—bigger than it looked on the outside. Four reception rooms in all, two office-cum-studies and a huge kitchen with quaint old-fashioned fittings that she liked on sight. Upstairs were six large bedrooms but only two bathrooms, which, Sandro informed her, would have to be put right before they could move in here permanently.

There had to be a catch to all of this, she told herself again. There just had to be—or why bring this beautiful place into the conflict at all? After all, he didn't need it to keep the pressure on her, because he was managing to do that very successfully without it!

So, she held herself tense and silent as they moved from room to room, letting him do the talking, waiting for him to get to the point and finally tell her what the catch was.

They had looked over the whole house and had come back to the hallway before he actually asked her a direct question. 'So?' he prompted. 'Do you like it?'

'I think it's delightful,' she replied. 'But I don't understand why you think I should *want* to live in a place like this?'

He didn't answer immediately. Instead he walked over to one of the windows and stood gazing outside for a while. He looked sombre suddenly, as though he was considering uttering something he wasn't sure was the right thing to say. Accordingly Joanna felt the muscles encasing her spine contract with tension.

'Molly told me that you used to live on a farm once,' he revealed. 'Until your grandfather died and your mother decided she did not want to take over his tenancy, and so she moved you all up to London to live.'

Molly had told Sandro that? Joanna was shocked. She hadn't been aware that Sandro and her sister had ever been close enough to talk about things like that!

'She said you used to love it there,' he continued, turning to watch the different expressions as they flickered across her face. 'She said you loved the clean air and wide-open spaces and the sense of freedom to come and go as you please. Apparently you had a horse of your own and used to ride him everywhere. She told me how much you missed it all once you were stuck in London...'

Silence. Joanna stood there in a dusty sunbeam while she came to terms with the disturbing fact that Sandro knew a lot more about her than she'd ever suspected he knew.

'Say something,' he prompted.

'Molly said an awful lot to you, by the sound of it,' was the only remark she could come up with.

He grimaced, hands doing their usual thing by sliding into his trouser pockets in a way that was supposed to be relaxed but which Joanna suspected meant he was the complete opposite.

'We used to meet,' he confessed. 'For lunch—perhaps once a month after you left me. I needed to know how you were coping and she was more than willing to talk about you...'

Tears washed across her eyes and stayed there, blurring out the dusty brown floor at her feet; a pain she couldn't quite interpret was tugging at her heartstrings. Grief for a much-missed Molly? Probably. Hurt for all those secret meetings she hadn't known had been going on between her sister and Sandro? Definitely. But, most of all, she felt dreadfully exposed again, as though nothing about her was sacred where Sandro and his obsession with her were concerned.

'Then...' he went on, and his voice sounded constrained now, enough to set Joanna moving restlessly, her arms wrapping themselves around her body so her fingers could pick tensely at the soft sleeves of her creamy top. 'A couple of days before I was due to fly out here to spend some time with my mother, because she had been ill and she seemed to need me more at that moment than you seemed ever likely to need me...'

He paused, she presumed it was to grimace at his own honesty, but she couldn't look at him to check that out, and, anyway, the tears were still blurring her vision.

'Molly called me up and asked me to meet her. She sounded—distressed,' he said. 'We met for lunch, and it was then that she told me what you had apparently only just told her, about what had happened to you and why you couldn't live with me. She asked me if it made a difference to how I felt about you,' he said, and then went on gruffly, 'I said, Of course it made a damned difference, but, for once, you were going to have to wait until I had given my mother the few weeks I had put aside for her to oversee her convalescence!'

Defiance, Joanna recognised. Oh, there had been a lot of angry defiance in those words just then.

'When I got back to London—' He had to stop a moment because his voice had broken, and Joanna squeezed her eyes tight shut because she knew what he was going to say next. 'You had both left the flat,' he continued. 'I could not bring myself to believe it at first, then I assumed that Molly must have told you what she had told me, and you had, predictably, made a run for it, because you couldn't stand the idea of my pursuing you again. In fact,' he concluded, 'I was so sure that was the case that I did not even bother checking any further than your flat, which is why I never got to hear about what happened to Molly.'

In other words he'd presumed the worst about her, Joanna noted hollowly. Just as she had presumed the worst about him.

'Now I want to make reparation for the last year, which must have been hell for you. And this,' he explained with a slow wave of one beautifully sculptured hand, 'is my way of making that reparation. I give you wide-open spaces, Joanna, and the freedom to enjoy it as you wish...'

The reparation was *his* reparation not *her* reparation? 'Y-you mean...?' she stammered out incredulously. 'You mean you've bought this beautiful place for me because you feel you owe me something?'

'Do I not?' he countered.

'No!' she cried 'You do not!'

'I will have to move main control of the bank back to Rome, of course,' he said, speaking right over her protest as if she hadn't voiced it. 'But I will install a full communications system here, for convenience, which will mean less commuting for me, so we can work at this place together...'

Joanna stared at him and couldn't even breathe through the pressure building in her breast. He believed she would be happy living in the country, so he had bought them a country estate to live on! And he was going to move his head operation back to Rome—again!

In other words, he was prepared to move heaven and earth to make this work for them—again.

'And what do you want, Sandro?' she asked him huskily. 'What is it you personally want from all of this for yourself?'

He shrugged, then smiled a wry kind of smile that thoroughly mocked whatever it was he had been going to say before he'd even bothered saying it. 'A wife who will be a wife to me would be nice.'

And that was all? A minor want like that? A perfectly justifiable want for any man, never mind a man like Sandro!

But, oh, good grief, it was like a mountainous obstacle to her!

'Oh, Sandro,' she sighed in shaken response, knowing she could never give him what he wanted. She had proved beyond all doubt this morning that she was incapable of being a proper wife to him! Which meant, therefore, that she could not accept anything else from him. 'Stop doing this!' she cried out in pained compulsion. 'Don't you see I'm not worth it? I don't even want it!'

'Then what do you want?' he demanded.

You, she thought hopelessly, and turned away from him so he wouldn't see that answer written in her eyes.

'No!' he objected, angry now, very angry, because once again she was letting him down with her inability to give him back what he needed from her. Striding towards her, he grabbed her arm and spun her back to face

him. 'You will stop hiding from me whenever we begin
to get close to the real truth!' he grated at her.

'I can't keep taking from you and giving nothing
back!' she cried in pained distress.

'Then give yourself to me,' he answered simply.

'I can't!' she choked. Good grief, did he never listen
to a word she said to him? 'I can't, damn it. *I can't!*'

He sighed, straightened his body as though he was
containing something very intense deep down inside
him, then unclipped his hands from her shoulders and
moved off towards the sunny front doorway.

'Come on,' he said to her over his shoulder. 'There is
a lot more to see yet outside. I think you will like the
stables...'

Joanna couldn't believe it! She stood there, exactly
where he had left her, and marvelled incredulously at
the stubborn way he was still completely ignoring anything she said to him that he didn't like!

In the end she followed him outside and let him show
her the gardens and the stable block, for which, he informed her, she was to choose her own stable of horses
once they'd made the house fit to move in to permanently. In a daze she let him guide her from one thing
to another, said nothing—thought nothing! Her mind had
shut down completely, as though someone—namely
Sandro—had turned it off for her because her thoughts
didn't suit him.

An hour after that they were back at the car, and for
one last time she tried to get through to him.
'Sandro—please!' she begged, 'Will you listen to me?'

'Not unless you are going to say something positive,'
he replied coolly.

'I positively know I am never going to be able to let
you make love to me,' she answered bluntly.

'Why not?' he challenged.

She didn't answer, her eyes lowering from his, her
lips pressed grimly shut.

'Still more ghosts to uncover, Joanna?' he prodded.

You are my ghost, she answered silently. You haunt my every breathing moment. 'I've faced the ghosts,' was what she said out loud. 'Without it changing anything.'

'No, Joanna,' Sandro responded. 'There are still some ghosts lingering here that I have not managed to uncover yet. But I will,' he vowed. 'I will find that person I once fell in love with. The person who once loved me in the same exquisite way, no matter what it takes to do it. And that,' he concluded, 'is what is called positive thinking, *cara*. Not that negative stuff you keep on throwing at me.'

'You're mad,' she sighed, her red-gold hair glinting in the sunlight as she sent him a look of weary frustration. 'You have to be—if you are this pig-headed!'

'You think me mad?' He laughed. 'No—no.' He denied the charge. 'For I can remember that what we had was so damned special only a madman would let it slip through his fingers—which I am not about to do!'

'You let it go once before,' she reminded him.

'But I did not know why you drove me to do so,' he countered. 'You let me believe it was my fault, something you could not stand about me! I could not overcome your physical aversion then, Joanna, but I can now, and I will,' he stated grimly. 'I'll overcome your sad determination to punish us both for something neither of us had any control over!'

With that, he turned and climbed into the car, leaving her to follow or stay as she felt fit. She followed, because she was heavily aware that she had no real choice about it.

No choice.

She almost laughed, except the situation warranted tears, not laughter.

He already had the engine running by the time she got in beside him, his dark expression set in stone and the atmosphere so bad now that neither of them made any attempt to ease it. They drove back down the cypress-lined driveway without another word passing between them.

She felt angry and guilty and cruel and petty. Maimed, that was what she was, she told herself bitterly. Maimed to the very roots of her persona if she could treat him as badly as this.

It was not a very pleasant thing to know about oneself.

That was why this relationship could never work for them. She would always be letting him down like this. Just as she had always let him down before.

So the gulf between them seemed to get even wider, and the antagonism to get so biting that Sandro curtly excused himself the moment they arrived back at the apartment late that afternoon, and disappeared behind a slammed door to his private study.

Joanna winced, recognising the sound from three years ago. This is it, she likened dejectedly; the slippery, sliding slope back into emotional carnage.

And it wasn't over yet. She was just coming out of her bedroom, after showering and changing into a cool cotton sundress, when she heard voices in the drawing room. With a sinking heart she recognised the voice of their visitor, and she gritted her teeth and made herself walk into the room.

Sandro and his mother were standing sharing softvoiced, angry words, by their tones. They were speaking in Italian, so Joanna had no idea what they were actually saying, but the moment they both noticed her standing there they clammed up so tightly that she knew they must have been discussing her.

'Mamma has just discovered we are here in Rome,' Sandro informed her coolly, 'and decided to pay us a visit.'

His mother winced, and Joanna understood her desire to do it. Sandro's voice had been sliced through with grating sarcasm.

'*Buona sera*, Joanna,' his mother greeted her, rather ruefully. She was a short, slender, very elegant creature, with dyed dark hair and her son's velvet brown eyes. Eyes that were fixed coolly on Joanna at the moment. 'It is good to see you again, my dear...'

Was it? Joanna didn't think so, going by the look in those eyes right at this moment. 'Thank you,' was all she said, stepping forward to allow their cheeks to brush in the expected Latin way of greeting. 'I w-was about to make some coffee,' she murmured, looking desperately for a way of escaping this awkward situation. 'Perhaps you would like to s-sit down while I go—'

She was already turning for the door when a telephone began ringing in Sandro's study. 'I need to answer that,' Sandro said grimly. 'You stay and talk to Mamma.'

Joanna stared at him in horror as he went striding by her. Don't you dare do this to me! her eyes pleaded furiously. He ignored her, still so angry with her that she supposed this was his way of getting his own back.

'Please, Joanna, come and sit by me and tell me what you have been doing with yourself since we last met.'

Oh, damn. Joanna's shoulders dropped, her bank of energy along with them. Turning with an air of dull fatalism, she made herself walk over to the sofa and sit down beside Sandro's mother.

'You are looking well,' his mother remarked politely.

'Thank you,' she replied again. 'And s-so are you,' she felt compelled to add. 'Sandro has been telling me that you've been ill recently.'

The older woman nodded. 'Last year it was necessary I underwent some open heart surgery,' she explained, with a small grimace that revealed a reluctant acceptance of her illness. 'Alessandro took me to Orvieto to convalesce afterwards. It is such a peaceful place to be, away from Rome's constant rush and noise, when one is feeling under the weather...'

'Yes.' Joanna nodded, her eyes glazing with a wistful understanding of what her mother-in-law meant.

'Of course,' his mother acknowledged. 'For you have just arrived back from visiting the old Campione estate. Alessandro was explaining why I could not reach him by telephone today. I discovered by pure accident, you see, that you were here with my son.'

And here it comes, Joanna noted, her spine straightening slightly, because she had a fairly good idea what was going to come next, like— What the hell do you think you're up to, disrupting my son's life a second time?

Yet it didn't come. 'You liked the estate?' Sandro's mother asked instead.

'Very much—who wouldn't?' Joanna found a stiff little smile from somewhere. 'It's such a beautiful place.'

The older woman nodded. 'Alessandro and I visited it several times while we were there. He was so very drawn by this idea, you see, that a country home could well be the lure he was searching for to coax you back to him.'

Joanna blinked. Sandro had been considering that beautiful place as far back as twelve months ago? She had believed it was a recent impulsive decision on his part.

'But of course,' his mother continued levelly, 'the best made plans can to go awry, even for a man like Alessandro. I was sorry to hear about the tragic death of your sister, Joanna,' she added gently. 'It must have come as a terrible blow to you.'

She knew about that too? Joanna's spine went a little straighter. 'It was at the time,' she agreed. 'But I am over it now.'

'Still…' Obviously not put off by Joanna's stiff tone, the older woman continued, 'It seems dreadfully fated that while my son was planning his campaign to reinstate

you as his wife, you were enduring such a terrible loss...
Do you believe in fate, Joanna?'

'I don't know,' she answered warily. 'I've never really
thought about it.'

'Do you believe in love, then?' the older woman persisted. 'Do you believe that a good, honest and true love
can conquer all, or do you think that even the best love
may always be fated to fall by the wayside, no matter
what the lovers try to do to hold onto it?'

'I don't think I understand what you're trying to say,'
Joanna replied carefully, while her eyes darted across the
room in the dubious hope that Sandro would reappear
and put a stop to this before it got out of hand.

But he didn't appear and, like her son, the mother was
obviously someone on a mission at the moment, because
she touched Joanna's hand to regain her attention. 'What
I am trying to ascertain, *cara*,' she said gently, 'is
whether you believe that your marriage has a better
chance at succeeding this time, or whether this is just a
sad case of Alessandro refusing to accept defeat.'

'We are working on it,' Joanna said tightly.

'The physical side?'

Joanna shot to her feet. So did Sandro's mother, her
hand closing around Joanna's wrist with a surprising
strength for such a slight person. 'I am not trying to
make trouble,' she asserted anxiously, making trouble
with every word she spoke. 'But—please, Joanna, you
have no *mamma* to talk to about these things! God
knows,' she murmured unsteadily, 'it cannot be easy for
you after what you have been through. But I do not want
to see Alessandro hurt as badly this time as he was the
last, because you could not—'

She stopped and swallowed. Joanna began to tremble
because it was beginning to hit her, really hit her, what
his mother was actually saying here.

'I would like to help, if I can.'

'No one can help.' Abruptly Joanna pulled her captured wrist free, her face turned to ice, her body cast in it. 'This is not your problem.'

'What's going on here?'

Joanna spun on her heel to stare at Sandro through eyes made of glass. 'You told her,' she accused him. 'I'll never forgive you.'

With that she went to stalk past him, but he stopped her by gripping her by the shoulders.

'Let me go,' she bit out in revulsion—the first true revulsion she had shown him since his return into her life.

'Mamma does not know it all,' he avowed. 'Only what Molly told me. I am only human, *cara*,' he added on a short sigh, when her icy expression did not alter. 'I needed to talk to someone I could trust about what had happened to us!'

It didn't matter. To Joanna, still too much had been said. 'It didn't happen to *us*, Sandro, it happened to me!'

'Us, Joanna,' he insisted grimly. 'What those animals did to you, they did to me also. And, like you, I have been paying the price for their actions ever since!'

'Well, you don't have to pay the price any more,' she said, 'because I am leaving here—even if that means I walk the streets of Rome for ever!'

'You think I will let you go?' he mocked. 'Simply because you are angry at what you see as my betrayal of a confidence?'

At last her cold eyes revealed life, flashing with anger. 'I trusted Molly to keep my confidence, but she told you,' she tightly pointed out. 'Molly trusted you to keep her confidence, but you told your mother. Who has your mother told, Sandro?' she demanded. 'How many of the great Bonetti family are by now whispering behind closed doors about the dreadful fate of your sad marriage to a ruined woman?'

'Oh—no, Joanna!' his mother put in anxiously. 'I have told no one! I would not!'

But Joanna wasn't listening; she had gone way beyond the point of listening to anything anyone had to say to her any more. 'I feel violated all over again, do you know that?'

Sandro let out a heavy sigh and tried to draw her closer to him, but she wasn't going to let him. Quite suddenly, she began to shake—shake violently. To shake with anger, horror and a soul-crushing self-revulsion that had always made up a large part of her emotional reaction to what had happened to her.

'Joanna, don't do this!' Sandro muttered, trying to once more draw her closer, but still she wasn't letting him. 'Damn it!' he cursed. 'Mamma—why could you not just leave well alone!'

'Sh-she's right, though, isn't she?' Joanna said, pushing her head up to gaze into those grim brown eyes that always seemed so angry now. 'I should not be doing this to you again. I keep trying to tell you that!'

'The only thing you are doing to me is hurting me because you hurt.'

'I am no good to you any more!'

'You will stop saying things like that!' he snapped. 'Because some animals took you against your will, that does not make you untouchable, Joanna!'

'But it does—don't you see?' she cried, her eyes bright, hot and painfully haunted. 'I had only one thing I could give to you, Sandro! One small thing that made everything perfect. Because you could give me the world where I had so little to offer you, except for that one s-small thing that you thought was so s-special. And they took it!' she sobbed, her voice lifting to a heart-wrenching shrillness. 'They stole the only thing I had that I could give to you! N-now I can't give myself at all!' she finished achingly. 'I can't do it, Sandro. I'm sorry, but I *just can't do it*!'

'Santa Maria?' Sandro's mother breathed in pained

understanding from somewhere beyond the heavy mists of Joanna's own helpless anguish.

Sandro said nothing. He just stood there in front of her with his lean dark features turned white. His mouth was clamped shut, his lips drawn inwards so there was barely an outline left on show. His jaw had locked and his eyes had gone so black they were like twin tunnels leading directly to his darkened soul. He tried to swallow but didn't quite manage it.

Above all, he was trembling—whether he was trembling with appalled comprehension at last, or trembling with sheer bloody anger was difficult to tell.

But Joanna knew she could not stay around to find out. She had to get out of there, away from the apartment, away from the hell it had all become. But, most of all, she had to get away from him.

Breaking free from his grip, she was suddenly off and running. Running before Sandro had a chance to react. Running into the hall and out of the apartment. Running into the waiting lift, where she stabbed an urgent finger at the console, then turned on shaking legs in time to glimpse Sandro angrily striding towards her as the doors closed firmly between them.

She heard his fist hit the solid door, heard him swearing and cursing until she was out of earshot. Then the doors were sliding open again and she was running again, out into the street as dusk was just beginning to turn everywhere a rich silken red, and still she kept going, on feet that seemed to have been given wings.

CHAPTER TEN

How far she got away from the building before Sandro eventually managed to catch up with her, Joanna didn't know. She had no idea where she was even running to! But she pulled to a panting halt when a familiar black car sped by and skidded to a screeching halt several yards in front of her.

Its door flew open even before the car engine had shuddered its last jolting breath, then Sandro was climbing angrily out.

Tall, lean, heart-rendingly handsome and excruciatingly special, he began striding towards her with that same look of whitened anger etched into his face.

He said not a word, his mouth nothing more than a thin, tight line, as he reached out and took a firm grip on her wrist, turned on his heel and began pulling her behind him back to the car.

His free hand tugged the passenger door open. He urged her inside, shut the door with a muted slam that made her wince, then was striding around the car's shining bonnet to climb in beside her.

His door slammed them in. Reaching out with a long finger, he touched a switch that sent all the locks shooting into their housing, then he just sat there, one hand clenched into a fist on his thigh, the other pressed into the line of his tightly held mouth, while Joanna sat beside him, gasping for breath after her wild bid for escape and sweating so badly that her skin glistened with it.

'I...'

'Don't!' he gritted. 'Don't say a bloody word.'

She blinked and was thoroughly silenced by the power

of emotion he'd infused into that command. In the midst
of that emotion, he started the car engine, threw it into
gear, then jettisoned them off down the road.

The journey back to his apartment was achieved so
quickly that Joanna wondered deliriously why she had
bothered to run at all! They jerked to a stop and he got
out, came round and opened her door to pull her out. He
didn't look at her, hadn't looked at her since the car
skewed to a halt in the road. He hauled her into the
building, then into the waiting lift.

They shot upwards. She didn't even notice, she was
so busy worrying what was coming next. He opened the
apartment door, hauled her inside there also, slammed
the door shut, then made a grim point of firmly locking
them in. Then and only then did he seem to pause to
take stock of the whole crazed, wretched experience.

But Joanna didn't feel like hanging around to wait for
whatever conclusions he eventually came to. She made
a second bolt for it, flying down the hall and into the
bedroom, hurriedly shutting the door behind her before
going to sink down weakly on the side of the bed, wishing the door had a lock on it so she could make sure she
kept him out.

But there was no lock, and she was trembling with
reaction now, shaken to the very core by her own wild,
naked confession and the tearing run that had followed
it.

'Oh, God,' she sobbed, and dropped her face into her
hands—only to fly jerkily to her feet again because she
could hear him just outside her door and she couldn't
face him yet; she just couldn't!

The bathroom door had a lock on it! she remembered,
and moved off on shaky legs towards it—

'Try it,' a super-grim voice behind her invited, 'and
watch me break it down if I have to.'

'I n-need a shower,' she improvised, tossing the sup-
posedly casual words over her shoulder so she did not

have to turn and face him. 'I'm sweating and the air-conditioning is on. It's ch-chilly in here.'

'What it is, *cara*,' Sandro drawled, 'is you on the run again. But, as you see, I am not going to let you. So you may as well turn and face me yourself, rather than have me make you do it.'

And he meant every silkily threatening word of it, Joanna acknowledged sinkingly. Sandro was that man on a mission again, and her innermost soul laid out for his inspection was that mission's goal.

'Y-your mother—'

'Is very relieved to know that I have you safely back here with me,' he inserted. 'And has gone home to recover from the whole wretched scene you threw!'

I threw! Joanna repeated in silent scorn. And who had instigated the wretched scene? His mother, that was who!

'Turn, Joanna.'

Her hand was at her aching eyes again, but almost instantly dropped to her side. Making a small fist, she grimly straightened her shoulders before she spun abruptly on her heel. 'Happy now?' she tossed at him defiantly.

'No,' he replied. 'You look dreadful.'

He didn't look too good himself, she noticed with a terrible ache inside her. His face was still pale, still drawn, his eyes too black, his lips still held in a thin, tight, angry line.

'I'm sorry,' she whispered, unable to stop herself.

As usual he wasn't impressed by the apology. 'Has it never occurred to you, *cara*, that there is a hell of a lot more to loving someone than the size of their bank balance?'

'I've never wanted your money!' She denied that implication hotly.

'Quite,' he said, throwing her into a mind-numbing confusion as to what he was trying to get at here!

Then she found out. 'As I never wanted your virginity,' he declared, watching almost detachedly as she went white at the very mention of the word. 'Although I do admit that once I believed I was getting it I felt honour-bound to treat such a gift with the respect it clearly deserved. No, don't you dare turn away from what I am saying here!' he rasped out, when she went to do just that. 'You will keep facing me and listen!' he commanded, levering himself away from the door to start towards her. 'You will listen, Joanna,' he gritted. 'As I had to stand and listen to your heart-rending little speech just now!'

'I knew you would never understand how I feel!' she cried, backing away as he came nearer.

'Oh, I understand that you truly believe I held your innocence in a higher regard than the love I felt for you!' he snapped. 'And you insult me with that opinion, do you know that? You insult what we had together and you insult the way I loved you!'

Fine words, three years after the event, Joanna thought bitterly. She could still remember the fuss he'd made about her virginity then—and the way he'd changed towards her! Goodnight pecks on the cheek, instead of long, passionate embraces! Holding her hand instead of letting his hands roam all over her!

In fact, she had begun to wonder if he would actually bring himself to take that precious virginity from her once it was his for the taking!

'And you're turning it all round to suit your own view of things again,' she threw angrily back at him. 'It is always how you feel, Sandro! How I let you down all the time—as if you think I don't already know exactly how badly I failed you!'

'Not with this virginity thing, you do not,' he denied. 'For what is a thin veil of skin in reality, *cara*? It is there for the practical purposes of protecting the female womb against infection and disease until the said female is ready to go forth and produce children. Nothing more—' he shrugged '—nothing less. Unless you are some kind of purity-obsessed barbarian, of course, which I am not,' he declared.

'But it was mine to bestow where I wanted to bestow it,' she reasoned shakily. 'And I wanted to give it to you!' It was a cry from the very heart of her. 'When they stole that right from me, they stole my special gift to you!'

'And once it was gone, it was gone for ever, Joanna,' Sandro grimly pointed out. 'Yet the importance you place upon it seems to suggest that once you had given this precious gift to me, you would have had nothing else left to give!'

'Which doesn't alter the truth, Sandro! That I find I cannot even think of letting you m-make love to me without it tearing me apart inside because of the loss of that gift!'

'You think I will miss it?' he demanded. 'That I will mourn its loss and think less of you for that loss?' He had the gall to laugh, albeit contemptuously. 'I would have thought it was damned obvious that I would rather be allowed to make love to my wife than live the bloody frustrating life I have been living without being allowed to touch her!'

'I told you you wouldn't understand,' she sighed out shakily.

'Oh, I understand a whole lot more than you give me credit for,' he came right back. 'I understand very well that you are really nothing more than a very frightened virgin at heart.'

Joanna jumped, shocked and hurt by the interpretation.

'What those two animals did to you does not count,' he dismissed with a deriding flick of his hand. 'That was a mere technicality beside the real issue that keeps you in this pathetic state of high anxiety. And what is the real issue?' he proposed. *'You,'* he answered for himself. 'You have difficulty finding enough courage to give yourself to me. *Yourself*, Joanna,' he repeated forcefully. 'Your *virgin* self! The self you give freely to me—which is the real gift of love from one person to another. Not that fine veil of skin you set so much store by. And if you continue like this,' he concluded as he turned towards the door again, so obviously sick to death of her that it showed in every distasteful line on his face, 'then you are condemning us both to lot of misery,' he warned. 'Because you will be condemning me to a life of frustrating celibacy, and yourself to a life of guilt and anguish while you watch me suffer like that!'

'W-what do you mean?' she whispered, not liking at all what she suspected he was saying.

'Exactly what your horrified mind is telling you,' he replied. 'That this marriage is for life. I am not letting you push me out of it a second time. Unless, of course,' he tagged on grimly, as he pulled open the door, 'you cling so tenaciously to what is in effect a damned lost cause, I may decide it is more than time to let go of my own lost cause!'

Which so obviously meant her that Joanna just stood there staring as the door closed behind him, his words having had such a profound effect on her that she could barely draw in breath!

Lost cause? Was that what she was? Was that what this whole wretched state of affairs was really all about—a lost cause?

Her legs gave out, sinking her weakly onto the bed because she had suddenly realised that Sandro was oh, so right!

In her own case, what was gone was indisputably gone! Pining over its loss was never going to bring it back again!

She *had* been clinging to the principles of a long-lost cause! She truly *was* a frightened virgin at heart, afraid to give herself freely to the man she loved in case he took and found her wanting!

And what those two men had done to her *didn't* count, not any more.

It couldn't count, she realised suddenly, if she was going to salvage anything at all from this mess she had made of both her own and Sandro's lives!

Because that was something else he had been right about, namely, why should he continue clinging to something that was so clearly becoming his own lost cause?

Abruptly she was on her feet again, shivering, cold— so cold it struck at the very heart of her. Cold with fear. But this fear was different from the one she was used to feeling, because it came from a fear of losing, not the old fear of giving.

Sandro was beginning to see her as a lost cause. He was going to give up on her!

That was when the panic flared—again, not the old panic but a new panic, which set her moving jerkily towards the bathroom with the certain knowledge of what she had to do if she wanted to make things right between them ringing like a warning bell inside her head. It had her quickly stripping off and showering her clammy body. Had her hurriedly tugging a long white bathrobe over still damp skin with shaking fingers

She didn't know if she could carry it right through to its natural conclusion, but she was certainly going to try!

The rest of the apartment was quiet when she stepped out of her room, so quiet she began to fear that Sandro might well have left it altogether! That fear tagged itself on to the end of every other fear she was desperately trying to wage war with as, to the pulsing rhythm of her own tense heartbeat, she made herself walk down the hallway to the room she had not let herself enter in three long years.

Pressing anxious teeth into her trembling lower lip,

she reached for the door handle and made herself turn it.

Her eyes honed directly in on him the moment she stepped inside. It was such a relief to find him there that she never even noticed the once-daunting quality of high ceilings and grey-painted walls washed over with eau-de-nil and gold leafed features.

She didn't see the majestic bed, or recall that the last time she had been in this room she had enacted the kind of horrified scene that had left Sandro utterly shaken.

None of that seemed to matter any more, because he was all that mattered. This man who was standing there, staring out of the window, lost in his own grim train of thought. He had showered too, she noticed, his long lean body wrapped in a short white towelling bathrobe similar to her own.

He had heard her enter, because he was turning abruptly, his dark eyes still those two pinpoints of anger lancing into her, until he grimly hooded them over with his lids, closing her out.

Was it too late? Had she already left it too late to salvage this precious marriage of theirs? Her heart flipped over, all those fears and uncertainties centering on that closed, grim face, the knowledge of what she had to do next making her fingers tremble as they reached up to the knot that was holding her bathrobe in place.

The action stiffened his body slightly. His eyes flicked upwards to clash with hers in a question that brought a flood of heat rushing to her cheeks.

But she determinedly continued with what she was intending to do. Heart hammering, lungs tight, she let her fingers loosen the robe belt and slowly parted the heavy fabric, sliding it from her slender shoulders until its weight sent it falling from her body to land in a snowy heap around her feet.

Naked.

Married for three years, wildly in love for even longer than that, yet this was the first time she had stood in front of Sandro naked.

It was such a dramatic gesture. So in keeping with the dramatic way Joanna dealt with all situations in her life, be it love, fear, pleasure or trauma.

Which category this particular gesture fell into, she wasn't sure; she had a suspicion it was a mad tangle of all four emotions as she stood there, watching the way those long, lush lashes lowered over the dark burn in his eyes as they swept slowly over her, from satin-smooth shoulders to the high, firm thrust of her rounded breasts.

They responded by tightening, the rosebud tips stinging into prominent life under his hooded gaze. The silence in the room was stunning; neither moved, neither breathed as Sandro slid his gaze lower, over the slender ribcage that led to her narrow waist and flat stomach, where the hollow of her navel quivered slightly under stress. Then on, further on, down across the gentle swell of her hips to linger finally on the soft cluster of red-gold curls that defined the heart-shaped apex where her long, shapely thighs met with the very core of her sex.

That part of her began to throb softly, her bare toes curling in response. Did he understand what she was trying to do here? she wondered tensely. Did he see that she was trying to give back to him something she had taken away from him, right here in this very room three years ago?

His face told her nothing, nor his stone-still stance.

'I love you so much, Sandro,' she burst out anxiously. 'Please don't give up on me yet. At least let me try to be a proper wife to you!'

Nothing. He came back with nothing. And in the growing tension Joanna waited, exposed, vulnerable, achingly unsure of herself, breath held, heart pounding, soft lips parted and quivering, her whole person quivering like some helpless sacrifice standing there waiting to hear its final fate. His gaze drifted over her one more time, lowering, then lifting, lifting until at last he let his eyes clash with her eyes...

Then he sighed, the sound seeming to come from some deep, dark well inside him. 'Come here, you crazy mixed-up creature,' he commanded huskily.

Relief broke from her on a stifled sob, then she was across the room and throwing herself against him, feeling his arms close around her, wrapping her own arms tightly around him.

Their mouths met in a hot fuse of raging hunger. There was no in-between. With typical drama she had let go of all her old prejudices and now she was wild for him. The kiss went on and on, consuming them both, consuming the room and the air inside it until she felt as if there was only herself and Sandro left to hold the whole world together.

His hands were all over her, touching, stroking, learning—claiming what she was offering, accepting it as his for the taking at last.

Eager to learn, desperate to please, she matched him kiss for passionate kiss, caress for each agonisingly arousing caress, which saw the last of the barriers between them collapse as his robe fell from his own broad shoulders. Naked together at last. She leaned against him, pressing herself into the full hard, hot length of him.

It was a revelation: her skin seemed to sizzle in response, her senses coming vibrantly alive to rush hungrily to the surface with a need to grab their share of a new and glorious sensation. Her breasts pushed themselves into the silken whorls of dark hair that covered the rock-solid wall of his wonderful chest; her spine arched her closer to him so her hips could mould themselves to the rigid power of his hips.

She felt the force of his response answer everything she was feeling; felt the heavy pound of his heart against the press of her eager breasts; felt the full, throbbing rise of his passion push against her arching hips; felt his arms tighten round her as if he was afraid she might turn tail and run; felt a groan of impassioned agony roll through him and the sting of his heated breath as he broke their mouths apart so he could mutter something barely distinguishable in shaken reaction to the whole wild experience.

'*Bellisima,*' it sounded like. '*Bellisima...*'

Then their lips were fusing again, with an electric pleasure that had her arms hooking urgently around his neck to keep him locked in a heated embrace so intense that it left no room for the old ghosts to appear.

When he picked her up and carried her to the bed, she clung to him, allowing him no space to move away from her as they fell in a tangle of limbs onto the mattress, where it all continued with barely a pause.

'Slow down,' he muttered at one point. 'We should take this very slowly, step by step. It does not have to be a conflagration, *cara mia.*'

'Yes it does,' she argued, skimming her eager fingers over his tight satin shoulders and into that mat of crisp dark hair on his chest. 'We took it step by slow step last time and look what happened. You lost something that belonged to you and I lost my way.'

'You belong to me,' he murmured. 'It is all I have ever wanted, *cara.*'

She nodded. 'I understand that now. But don't hold back from me, Sandro, for fear of frightening me,' she begged him. 'I need you to overwhelm me, to give me no time to change my mind, because I still have this horrible fear that at the final moment I am going to let you down again!'

She didn't let him down. She enchanted him. She made him fall in love with her ten times over.

'You have to stop that,' he murmured, gently removing her stroking fingers from where they were causing such havoc.

'Why?' she asked guilelessly, moving her hands to some other part of him she had already learned gave him pleasure.

'This is why,' he laughed softly, and ran his finger into the warm, moist crevice of her body that set her gasping while he lay beside her, watching her catch fire for him, watching her respond in complete abandonment to what he was making her feel.

It moved him—moved him fiercely to see how completely she was giving herself over to him. It was as if someone had opened a box containing all her stifled emotions and now they were out and flying free: no inhibition, just pure sensual freedom.

And it was all for him.

'Sandro,' she gasped, and he knew exactly why. But now it was his turn to feel uncertain, his turn to worry that he might just be the one to let her down.

Maybe she sensed that, maybe she knew that there was more at stake here than just her own old feelings of inadequacy. She had treated him too badly, and for too long, for those feelings of rejection to simply melt away.

Her eyes fluttered open and her hands reached up to mould his flushed, dark, passion-intense features. 'If you don't do it, I'll die,' she warned him softly.

Another laugh broke from him, gruff and rueful, maybe even a little shaken, as he shifted his body over hers, letting her feel his weight, the power of his passion, before he made that vital contact and began to push slowly, slowly inside her.

She was hot and she was tight, the untutored muscles of her pulsing silk sheath closing all around him as her slender body arched on a fierce intake of air; then— nothing.

She simply stopped breathing, her body held in a state of complete suspension that made him pause, his dark eyes fixing on her worriedly because he couldn't tell why she was responding like this.

'*Cara?*' he murmured in a thick-voiced question. 'Do I hurt you?'

She couldn't answer, was too thoroughly lost in the whole new experience. The feel of him, hard and strong and so completely filling her. The heat of him, mingling with her own burning heat, fusing them together as if to make them one entity. The very intimate scent of him, blending so perfectly with the scent of herself. And, most exquisite of all, the clear, sharp, sparkling knowledge that here she was, joined at last with this man she loved so much.

It was wonderful, like being set free of every single constraint that life had had to offer. On a sudden sunburst of unrestrained triumph, she laughed, her arms wrapping around his neck, her long legs wrapping themselves around his lean tight hips.

'I feel you, Sandro,' she confided in silken wonder. 'I can feel you throbbing deep inside me.'

The words moved him. Emotionally they moved him, sending the air rushing from his lungs on a shaken gasp. Physically they moved him, adding extra substance to his masculine potency. In the next moment he was kissing her, long and deeply, his tongue matching the powerful thrust of his body as he began to move, merging both acts into one glorious experience that held her completely captivated in its exciting thrall.

Then the sun-burst taking place inside her was no longer one of mere triumph, but a sun-burst of sensation—pure, sexual sensation. It opened like a budding flower, spreading its petals wider and wider on the rippling winds of an incredible pleasure, until—on a sharp indrawn gasp—she burst forth into full bloom, those delicate petals of sensation quivering out to encompass every nerve-end, every corner of her acutely responsive flesh.

Above her, Sandro was trembling with the constraint it was costing him to make this happen for her. With his hot mouth buried in her throat he moved on her, inside her, all around her. On fire, as she was on fire, so ultra-sensitised to every muscle pulse it was almost an agony to complete each sensual thrust of his body.

When her fingers caressed him, he shivered—not with cold, but with excruciating pleasure. When she kissed him, he groaned in anguish, but urgently kissed her back. But when the flower-burst began to happen inside her, he stopped moving altogether, watched her begin to bloom, felt the initial quivers of that final sensation take fierce hold of her, and with smooth, slow, careful timing, he guided her into that earth-shattering climax. Then he felt his own sun-burst begin to grow ever stronger, but only when she leapt did he give in to it; only when she cried out his name did he let go.

Reparation. It was his own reparation to hear the woman he loved so much crying out his name at this point of intense exaltation.

After that, everything splintered into a wild electric storm of pure feeling.

And neither had let the other down. Both lay there, still clasped tightly together in the prolonged and powerful aftermath, unable to move, their two hearts pounding as one.

'OK?' Sandro murmured when he could manage to speak at all, pushing up on his forearms so he could lay slightly trembling fingers against her flushed, damp cheek.

For an answer she kissed the hand, because it was impossible for her to use her voice yet. The biggest obstacle in her life had been surmounted at last and she was no longer a virgin—not in heart, not in mind, and definitely not in body.

'They were pretty inadequate, weren't they?' she whispered eventually.

'Who?' he demanded, already stiffening because he sensed rejection on the way.

'Those animals,' she explained, and opened her love-enriched blue eyes to gaze in wonder up at him. 'They had no idea what this is really all about.'

She thought he might get angry, was aware that he had a right to be angry with her for bringing that incident up at such a special moment. But Sandro was Italian, and Italian men were by nature very macho. He grinned—the kind of lazily smug grin that was ready to accept a compliment even if it was a very back-handed one.

'See what you have been missing out on all of these years?' he said arrogantly. 'Now, perhaps, I will get a little respect around here.'

'Ah,' she said, and suddenly the old Joanna was looking up at him, the blue-eyed, saucy minx he had first fallen in love with. 'But can you repeat the performance?' she challenged him. 'That's what I want to know.'

He repeated it, several times in fact, during that long, dark, steamy night.

The next morning she awoke to find herself curled around him. His arm was resting in the hollow of her waist, just below her ribcage, and his other was beneath her pillow, beneath her head, long fingers tangled amongst the tumbled silk flow of her hair.

She had never seen him look so wonderful, or so content, and she lay there for ages just gazing at him, basking in the full, glorious beauty of what they had shared the night before.

Then another need began to demand supremacy. Hunger pangs bit at her with a ravenousness she hadn't felt in days, weeks, months—years! She got up, stealthily sliding herself away from him so she wouldn't wake him, before padding softly across the bedroom with the intention of going to her old room to get dressed.

Then she spied his discarded tee shirt, lying where he must have angrily tossed it the night before, half on the back of an upright chair, half trailing on the floor. Sheer impulse made her snatch it up and take it with her out of the room.

She pulled it on over her head. It was huge, the hemline reaching well down her slender thighs. Grinning to herself, she continued on her way to the kitchen with her bare feet pressing into the cool mosaic tiling floor, aware of every tiny nook and cranny. In fact, she felt so super-sensitive to everything that even the brush of the soft, smooth cotton across her breasts was unutterably electrifying.

Freedom, that was what all this elation was, she recognised. She felt as if she'd been set free from eternal bondage. Reborn overnight into a completely different person.

A person who could even hum happily to herself while she prepared freshly squeezed orange juice to have with her breakfast of hot buttered toast.

'You sound cheerful,' a deep voice said.

She turned from what she was doing to find him leaning in the open doorway. He had already taken a shower and shaved, and he was wearing a pair of old boxer shorts and nothing else—except for the short-stemmed red rose he had stuck into the elasticated waistband.

Her senses began to sizzle, memories of the night before surging up like a fire to almost engulf her. This man, she thought breathlessly, this wonderful, sexy, dynamic man—is *my* lover!

My lover.

Possession gushed through her, plus a fierce sense of heart-bursting pride and a far more unrighteous sense of feline power—for, no matter how incredible he had made her feel last night, Joanna knew without a doubt that Sandro had felt it all just as deeply.

It was that same sense of power that brought on the very provocative response he received from her.

'Nice legs,' was all she remarked, before turning casually back to what she had been doing with a pile of fresh oranges and a juice-squeezer, deliberately ignoring the rose—just as she'd used to do.

She heard him move, felt the tingle of anticipation begin at her toes and start to run through her as his bare feet brought him to stand behind her. His hands slid around her waist and his dark head bent to nuzzle her nape, making her smile as she tilted her own head to give him better access.

'Mmm, this is the life,' he murmured. 'My sexy wife smelling of oranges and wearing my cast-off shirt.'

She turned within his arms so she was facing him. 'Here,' she said, and held her sticky fingers up for him to suck clean.

He did so quite happily, while his eyes held onto hers, filled with dark, lazy promises. But, for all her nonchalance, she felt a shy blush coming on, and she lowered her gaze to watch her slicked fingers collect the rose from the waistband of his shorts.

'Where do you keep producing these from?' she asked curiously.

'Secret,' he said. Then he was suddenly very serious. 'No more ghosts left now?' he questioned gently.

She shook her head, smoothing the deep red rose across her lips, then absently doing the same thing with it down the centre of his hair-roughened chest. 'Do you forgive me for the hell I've put you through?' she countered.

'There is nothing to forgive,' he said. 'You were in trauma. It closed you in behind a wall no one else could get through. I tried. Molly tried. And, although we did not understand why you were like you were, we were perceptive enough to realise something pretty dreadful must have happened to you to change you so radically, what seemed like overnight.'

'Did you ever guess at the truth?'

'I considered it as the most logical option,' he said. 'But, as you yourself pointed out, you had no cuts, no bruises, no evidence that pointed to a physical assault on your person...'

She shivered, then sighed and moved closer to him, so she could wrap her arms tightly round him. 'I want to forget it now,' she whispered sadly.

'Sure,' he agreed. 'Why not? Three years is more than long enough to let something as bad as that obsess your mind.'

'And today is the—fourth day of my new life,' she said, lifting her face so she could smile at him. 'What shall we do with it?'

His eyes began to gleam. She blushed again.

'Are you insatiable or what?' she chided.

'With you, satiation holds no bounds,' he murmured huskily. 'And I have three long years of wretched celibacy to catch up on.'

'Oh, Sandro—no!' she groaned in remorseful protest.

He actually looked shocked at her response. 'You think I would accept less than the best?' he demanded.

'But you told me you had a mistress!' she cried.

'You would have preferred it if I had used another woman as a substitute for you?'

'No,' she confessed huskily. 'But I would have understood it if you had done.'

'My pride may have demanded I mention a mistress,' he ruefully conceded, 'but I could not even bring myself to look at another women—never mind fancy one! But—hell,' he added on a small sigh, 'I was bitter about it. Especially during this last year, when you had disappeared altogether. I felt you had stripped me clean of my ability to be a man, *amore*,' he disclosed heavily. 'It was not a nice feeling, I promise you!'

'I do love you so,' Joanna informed him anxiously. 'I never wanted to treat you like that; I just couldn't help myself!'

'I was actually beginning to convince myself that I was much better off without you when you called,' he admitted.

Joanna groaned and hugged him tightly, in case he might decide he was still better off without her—in which case it would be her turn to refuse to let go!

'But the moment I heard your voice on the telephone it was as if something inside me caught alight,' he went on softly. 'I felt alive again suddenly—bursting with it, sizzling with it. So much so that even before you arrived at my place of work I had decided that you were never going to escape me again, even if I had to imprison you to keep you there! Then I was going to chip away at every last damned bloody stone in the wall you stood behind until I found the woman I fell in love with!'

'She's here,' Joanna assured him quickly.

He glanced down into her brimming blue eyes. 'All of her?'

'Yes.'

'Then let's go back to bed,' he said, reaching behind him to capture her hands so he could pull her with him out of the kitchen.

'But what about breakfast?' she protested. 'I'm hungry! I was just going to make you—'

'I've had mine,' he inserted arrogantly. 'I licked it from your fingers.'

Then they were inside his bedroom and the door was closing, and his hands were already beneath the shirt-hem and sliding it upwards and over her head, stripping her clear of any barriers.

His eyes glowed over her slender, pale, beautifully proportioned body, with its high, thrusting breasts and its intensely alluring cluster of dark gold between her thighs.

'You are so lovely you make my heart ache,' he told her huskily.

'So are you,' Joanna said, holding her arms up to collect him in. 'All my dreams come true.'

Passion

**Looking for stories that *sizzle*?
Wanting a read that has a little
extra *spice*?**

**Harlequin Presents® is thrilled
to bring you romances that
turn up the heat!**

In March 1999 look out for:

***The Marriage Surrender*
by Michelle Reid**
Harlequin Presents #2014

Every other month throughout 1999,
there'll be a **PRESENTS PASSION** book by one
of your favorite authors: Miranda Lee,
Helen Bianchin, Sara Craven and Michelle Reid!

*Pick up a PRESENTS PASSION—
where **seduction** is guaranteed!*

Available wherever Harlequin books are sold.

HARLEQUIN®
Makes any time special ™

Look us up on-line at: http://www.romance.net

HPPAS1-R

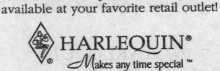

Coming Next Month

THE BEST HAS JUST GOTTEN BETTER!

#2019 PACIFIC HEAT Anne Mather
Olivia was staying with famous film star Diane Haran to
write her biography, despite the fact that Diane had stolen
Olivia's husband. Now Olivia planned to steal Diane's lover,
Joe Castellano, by seduction...for revenge!

#2020 THE MARRIAGE DECIDER Emma Darcy
Amy had finally succumbed to a night of combustible passion
with her impossibly handsome boss, Jake Carter. Now things
were back to business as usual; he was still a determined
bachelor...and she was pregnant....

#2021 A VERY PRIVATE REVENGE Helen Brooks
Tamar wanted her revenge on Jed Cannon, the notorious
playboy who'd hurt her cousin. She'd planned to seduce him,
then callously jilt him—but her plan went terribly wrong:
soon it was marriage she wanted, not vengeance!

**#2022 THE UNEXPECTED FATHER Kathryn Ross
(Expecting!)**
Mom-to-be Samantha Walker was looking forward to facing
her new life alone—but then she met the ruggedly
handsome Josh Hamilton. But would they ever be able to
overcome their difficult pasts and become a real family?

**#2023 ONE HUSBAND REQUIRED! Sharon Kendrick
(Wanted: One Wedding Dress)**
Ross Sheridan didn't know that his secretary, Ursula O'Neill,
was in love with him until his nine-year-old daughter, Katie,
played matchmaker.... Then it was only a matter of time
before Katie was Ross and Ursula's bridesmaid!

#2024 WEDDING FEVER Lee Wilkinson
Raine had fallen in love with Nick Marlowe, not knowing the
brooding American was anything but available. Years later,
she was just about to marry another man when Nick walked
back into Raine's life. And this time, he *was* single!